The Horse Trader

When Harry Rodriguez's wife and son died a terrible death, he decided to head out for pastures new. First off he met a couple of decent kids, but they were soon killed by Slim Loxton and his gang after they had kidnapped Kate Battersby off a stage.

Now everyone was playing for high stakes indeed. Harry met a card-sharp by the name of Brett Halliday and together they determined to rescue Kate Battersby.

But this was a formidable task, and before it could be achieved much lead would fly.

By the same author

Summer of the Gun

P

The Horse
Trader

BRENDAN FAGAN

A Black Horse Western

ROBERT HALE · LONDON

© Brendan Fagan 2001
First published in Great Britain 2001

ISBN 0 7090 7017 9

Robert Hale Limited
Clerkenwell House
Clerkenwell Green
London EC1R 0HT

Typeset by
Derek Doyle & Associates, Liverpool.
Printed and bound in Great Britain by
Antony Rowe Limited, Wiltshire

ONE

From the top of the hill Harry Rodriguez watched the tragedy unfold. A tragedy that he was powerless to prevent, and that involved his son, Charlie. Charlie had ridden too near the herd of wild horses. Suddenly, a black stallion turned on the boy's pony and ran at it. The pony took fright and reared. Harry's hands tightened and became white as he gripped the leathers of his horse. A scream of anguish stuck in his throat. Charlie, white faced with terror, slid out of the saddle and fell to the ground, For a few seconds he lay stunned, the breath knocked from his body. The pony backed towards him and struck him on the head with a hoof.

The stallion came on, driving the pony before it. The pony turned and fled as Charlie struggled to his feet. Tears ran down his face. The stallion reared and brought its forelegs down on the boy's head.

5

Shirley Rodriguez was crossing the yard from the cabin to the well that Harry had dug. A sudden pain in her head blinded her. She dropped the pail, clutched at her throat, and fainted.

Harry rowelled his horse and galloped down the slope. The stallion was readying itself for another lunge at the boy's head. Drawing his revolver, Harry fired two shots at the stallion. The wild horse stopped, and snorted at the air. Then it turned and galloped towards the hills.

Harry rode to where the boy lay bleeding. Sliding out of the saddle, he dropped to his knees and cradled Charlie in his arms. He did not have to be told that it was too late. What was he going to tell Shirley? The blood was matted in Charlie's thick black hair. In a daze, Harry gently picked him up. He caught at the leathers of his horse. He mounted and rode towards the cabin. As he rode into the yard, the cabin door banged in the rising wind. Uneasily, Harry looked round. He looked towards the well, and saw a bundle lying in the fading light. He could not see what it was. He called out for Shirley. She did not answer. The cabin door banged again. He looked again at the bundle lying by the well. A sudden thought ran through his mind. Gigging the horse over to the well, he dismounted and saw Shirley lying in a pool of her own blood.

The sobs racked his body, sending a shudder through it. Then for a while he was silent and still, as though there was nothing left in him. The wind rose steadily. He lurched over to the cabin and staggered inside. Instinct drove him so that he did not have to light the lamp. In a drawer he found a bottle of whiskey. Pulling the cork out with his teeth he spat it across the room and put the bottle to his lips. The burning liquid offered him no comfort. He pulled the bottle away so that he could take a breath. He put it to his mouth again, and tilted his head back. He only stopped drinking when the bottle was empty. Half-drunk with the grief and the whiskey, he lurched to the bed and collapsed across it. He slept until daybreak.

When he awoke, the bright sun was shining directly in his face. His mouth was dry and hot. Harry looked round. There was no sign of Shirley or Charlie. Maybe they were outside feeding the horses or fixing the fence. Maybe. Deep in his soul, he knew they were not. His head was thick and sore. He got up from the bed. They were both outside where he had left them. Their faces pale in death.

Harry went over to touch them just to make sure. Shirley, made ugly by the pain she had suffered, stared up at him. Harry moaned again as he looked at them. He knew that he could not leave them where they lay. Shirley's favourite spot was behind the cabin where she used to sit looking up at the hills. Charlie had come to like it down by the creek. Harry had planned to take him down there and teach him to fish.

The thought reminded Harry of how hard they had tried for a child and how they had finally succeeded. He could remember the night of the storm when Doc Lassiter had come out to deliver Charlie. He would never forget Shirley's cries of anguish through the long hours of the night. He had sat on the porch watching the lightning rip the black sky. He had listened to the rain battering at the shelter that he had put up for the horses.

Finally, there had come a plaintive cry as Charlie entered the world. Doc Lassiter had asked Harry to come into the cabin. Shirley lay on the bed, her face and forehead shining with sweat, her hair plastered down against her skull.

'I know how hard you've bin trying for a child,' Doc Lassiter had started by saying. Harry had detected something in his voice. 'Well you've got a healthy boy, but there ain't gonna be any more. If there are they'll kill her.'

Harry shrugged. In one sense he had been relieved, but in another, he was unhappy. He had come from a big family and he and Shirley had wanted a big family themselves. That was how things went, he had told himself. Now, he was going to have to bury them both.

Harry went over to the cabin and found a shovel. Going outside again, he looked round trying to find a place for them both. Wherever he put them to rest, he would have to see them every day. He had made his decision, Gently, he carried Shirley into the cabin and laid her on the bed. Then he went outside and got Charlie and put him on the bed in his room.

Taking two lamps, Harry filled them with kerosene and lit the wick. On the veranda he hesitated for a moment, then threw the lamps through the window. He had waited until the flames had taken a good hold, then ridden out without looking back.

TWO

Beaver was a town that had started up by accident. A trapper had been out setting his traps one day, when he had noticed something shining in the water. When he had finished examining it, he drew his revolver, and fired it into the air. He threw his hat up into the crisp air and let out whoop that woke up everybody in the next county.

It did not take him long to get to the nearest assay office and file a claim. Soon there was a steady stream of people heading up into the high country. Not many of them got rich quick or slow, but a heap of them realized there were other ways of making money, besides panning or digging for it.

Harry Rodriguez rode into Beaver one night, six months after he had burned his cabin, and his old way of life along with it. He hauled up outside the livery stable and waited for the whiskered oldster to come out to him.

'I'm looking for somewhere for my horse and myself to sleep,' he said to the old man.

'Reckon you can stay here, if you don't mind the smell of horses,' the old man said to him.

Harry laughed as he passed over the leathers. Digging the money out of his pocket, he handed it to the old man. He didn't have too much. At least, not where anybody would think of looking for it.

'I'll feed him and bed him down for you,' the old man said. 'You can bed yourself down over there.' He pointed to a warm-looking corner.

'Just one more thing,' Harry said.

'What'll that be?' the old man asked.

'Where do you figger I can get something to eat, without it costing me an' arm an' a leg?'

Grinning, the old man led him outside and pointed to a new part of town.

'There's a place called Madam Reno's. She can fix you up with some grub. It ain't great, but you can eat it without getting poisoned. It's opposite the Brandy Bottle saloon. You can't miss either of 'em.'

Harry waved his thanks and headed out for Madam Reno's. The ground was hard and dry. A cold wind was coming out of the east. Harry yawned and rubbed his aching stomach. He thought about the last time that he had eaten a hot meal: a week back on the trail, chasing a passel of wild horses.

Madam Reno's was the brightest of the eating

places on the block. Like the old man said, it was just opposite the Brandy Bottle. It sounded a pretty lively place.

He glanced through the window into the café. It was full, but there was one table standing empty at the back. He went inside and was hit by the smell of the food being cooked. His mouth started to water. Harry waited a few minutes for a waitress to come over. She was awfully young and awfully pretty.

'What have you got?' Harry asked her, when he had sat down.

'Potatoes, beef and gravy,' she said, with a smile.

'Anythin' else?'

'Gravy, potatoes and beef.'

'I guess it's gonna have to be potatoes, beef and gravy.'

The waitress walked away. Harry leaned back in his chair. The place was full of gold hunters. The girl came back a few minutes later with his food. Harry watched as the steam rose from it. The beef and potatoes smelled well-done. The girl put the food down in front of him. Then she took a set of eating irons out of her apron pocket and gave them to him.

'Enjoy your food,' she said to him, and went off to wait on another table. The first mouthful told Harry that the liveryman's advice had been good. He ate quickly, grateful for not having to make

conversation while he ate. It was not long before
his knife was scraping at the bottom of his plate.
Swallowing the last few mouthfuls, he belched
quietly and looked round for the waitress.

'Seems like you enjoyed that,' she said with a
smile.

'You got any pie to follow that down?' Harry
asked as he wrestled a piece of beef from between
his teeth.

'Sure have,' she told him and hurried off to get it.

The service was sure prompt in Madam Reno's,
Harry thought as she came back holding a pot of
coffee and a plate with a hunk of pie on it. The pie
was as good as the rest of the stuff, and it soon
disappeared. The coffee followed the food. Harry
loosened his belt and built himself a stogie, then
fished out the payment for his meal.

'Any saloons round here you can recommend?'
he asked.

'There's a dozen round here,' the girl replied.
'The one I'd recommend is just outside. It's the
Brandy Bottle. You must have passed it if you
came from the livery stable.'

'Yeah, I did,' Harry told her. He got up from the
table and left a tip for the girl.

Outside, the night was chilly. Music and shouting came from the saloons. Harry built himself
another stogie and strolled across the street. He
pushed through the batwings. The smoke and
music struck him as he went in.

Along the back wall ran the bar with customers three-deep at it. To his left was a stage with half a dozen girls dancing on it. They were doing a high-stepping dance to the accompaniment of a honky-tonk piano. They kicked their legs high, much to the appreciation of the customers, and let out a string of wild yells. Picking his way through the tables of card players, Harry pushed his way to the bar.

'What'll it be?' the barkeep asked.

'Beer,' Harry told him, and leaned on the bar while he was waiting for his beer. The gaming tables were full. There were a variety of players. Professional gamblers, drifters, ranch-hands, and a couple of gunmen. He gave the barkeep his money, and drifted into the playing area. Harry had never been a gambling man, and he didn't know why he was in there. He drifted in and out among the tables, only half-watching the games.

For a few minutes he watched a game start between a couple of greenhorn kids, a professional gambler and a drifter. The gambler was making the cards skitter across the green baize like they were on an ice rink. When he picked up his cards, Harry could see that he had a full house. The two green kids bet recklessly, the drifter folded and the gambler raked in the greenbacks.

He dealt a second hand with the same result. A few wild bets from the kids, and the drifter folded again. The gamblers well-cared-for hands raked in his winnings.

'Say, Frank,' one of the kids asked languidly, settling himself back in the chair. 'How many of them fancy court cards has Mister Slippery Fingers got up his sleeve?'

'I was just wonderin' that myself brother Billy,' came the reply.

The noise in the vicinity of the table died away.

'I say we find out,' Billy said. They both reached across the table, and hooked their hands round the lapels of the gambler's jacket. A moment later both boys landed their fists in his face, flattening his nose and sending blood squirting in every direction.

Harry tried to move away from the fight, but a bear of a man pulled him round. The man pulled back his fist to hit Harry, but Harry's foot landed in his shin. The man let go of Harry and screamed out with pain. Harry landed a blow to his open mouth. The girls on the stage were screaming and doing their best to get out of the way. Tables went over, and money was scattered all over the floor. Suddenly, there was the dull boom of a shotgun. Straight away a hush fell over the saloon.

Getting up from the floor, Harry could see three men with stars on their vests. They were standing just inside the saloon. One of them was holding a smoking shotgun.

'The party's over boys,' the sheriff said.

He broke open the shotgun and thumbed in a fresh shell.

'Judge Willet ain't gonna be too pleased to see you. He's got a new whore down there and he didn't want to be disturbed.'

From the look on the sheriff's face Harry guessed that Judge Willet would have something to say to him at some time or other.

'Now git yourselves formed up in a snake outside while we get down to the judge's house.'

The sheriff turned to the nearest deputy.

'Hank, you get yourself out there. Make sure none of these boys takes it into their heads to hightail it out of town.'

'Anythin' you say, Brad,' Hank said, and went outside.

'Mitch, bring up the rear. We don't want to be losing any of these boys.'

'Right, boss,' the moustachioed deputy replied.

'OK. The rest of you boys outside – now.' Brad gestured for them to go for the batwings.

Harry fell into line. His head was aching from the blow. The two boys and the gambler, who had started the ruckus, followed behind Harry.

When they got out into the street, it looked like the whole town had turned out to watch the show. As soon as they started down the boardwalk, there came a chorus of catcalls and jeers like nothing that Harry had ever heard before. Harry felt himself reddening under the jeering.

'Maybe this will bring them to their senses faster than any fines would,' Mitch called out.

They walked along the boardwalk for a while, then Harry heard Hank call out, 'Left here boys.'

The catcalling and jeering followed them down a second street as it had done in the first. They went on down the street, until they got to the edge of the town where the houses became a mite more prosperous-looking.

'OK. We're there,' Brad called out and headed for the front of the column. He pushed open a gate that smelled of fresh paint and went down the path to the door. He knocked loudly. A light came on in the upstairs room and a window slid open. Harry could make out the white-haired head of an old man sticking out of the window.

'What's going on down there?' the old man yelled. Harry figured it must be Judge Willet.

'Got some custom for you, Judge,' Brad called up to him.

'Damn it. What kinda custom?' the judge shouted back.

'The payin' kind,' Brad answered.

'Oh that kind.'

Harry noticed the tone of the judge's voice mellowed more than a mite when he heard the words 'payin' kind'.

'Just give me a couple of minutes while I make myself decent, then you can bring them in.' With that the window slammed shut.

Brad came out to the men. 'Hold it there. I don't think His Honour has finished with his whore yet.'

The men along the path sounded disgruntled, but there wasn't much they could do about it with three men holding shotguns on them.

When the window opened again, Harry saw the white head sticking out.

'Ready for you now, boys,' Judge Willet called out.

'You heard the judge,' Brad said.

The single file of men walked up the path. As they reached the porch, a light came on in the hall. The front door opened. With Brad heading up the column they trooped into the house. At the bottom of the corridor, lit with kerosene lamps, stood a table with a high chair behind it. Looking over in front of him, Harry could see what appeared to be a ledger on the table. There was a quill pen and an inkstand beside it. He guessed that the white lump of flesh sitting in the chair was Judge Willet.

'OK, boys,' the judge began. 'This is my court and what I say goes.'

A mumble of assent came from the men. The judge rapped on the table with his gavel.

'OK, Brad, bring the first one in,' Willet said, and pounded the desk again.

Brad led the first man out of the line. He was a big, hulking miner, who Harry had seen earlier throwing a table in the saloon.

The sheriff and the judge got their heads together for a minute, then the judge said, 'Fifty dollars,' and banged his gavel.

The miner started to protest, but the judge cut him short. 'Could make it one hundred for contempt of court.'

The miner's face turned white, then he said, 'OK.'

Judge Willet's pen scratched something in the ledger. He took the money from the miner, and dropped it in a box at the side of the ledger. The miner scowled, then left the house. It went on in the same way for a spell, with the fines being paid and the money being tossed into the box.

When it came his turn, Harry decided not to argue. When he was called to the table, the judge and the sheriff got their heads together. The judge looked up and banged his gavel.

'Fifty dollars,' he said.

Harry pulled off his battered hat, and counted the money from the inside of it. He watched with growing resentment as the money dropped into the box. He could see where the judge got the money to pay for his new house.

'Something the matter, bud?' the sheriff asked him giving him a light dig in the ribs with the shotgun.

'No – nothing, Sheriff,' Harry scowled as he folded the rest of his money and put it back in his hat.

'Then you'd better be on your way unless you want to pay another fifty dollars for contempt of court,' the sheriff added.

'No, I guess I'll pass on that one,' the horse trader said quietly and turned towards the door.

'You gonna wait fer us?' Frank caught his sleeve as he went past. 'Me an' Billy figured we owe you a drink or somethin'. I mean we think you must have spotted what Mister Slippery Fingers was up to at the same time as us.'

Harry thought for a moment, then said, 'Sure why not? There must be other saloons that'll serve us drinks. Anyway, you get yourselves sorted out an' I'll wait for you.'

Frank went up to the judge's table and watched as the sheriff and the judge swapped tales.

'Fifty dollars,' the judge said, holding out his hand.

Harry saw the boy's face pale. 'I ain't got fifty dollars,' he said.

'Too bad. In that case you can spend a month working it off on my claim. You might even get a bonus, if you work real hard. You say that's his brother, Sheriff?'

'That's his brother,' Brad told the judge.

'Well, assuming you've got no money either, the same goes for you. A month digging on my claim and a bonus if you work real hard.' The judge slammed his gavel down on the desk.

The two boys looked stunned.

'We've got different plans for ourselves,' Billy blurted out.

The sheriff grinned at them. 'You're talking

yourselves into another month without the bonus.'

The sentence outraged Harry because the fines were going into the judge and lawman's pockets. He took a breath and made a mental calculation. He had enough to pay the boys' fines, and there was a last reserve in his saddle-bag at the livery.

Harry took a step forward. 'I'll give you boys a hand,' he said.

'How?' Billy asked.

'I'll pay your fines, but you've got to do some work for me,' he said.

Frank cocked his head and looked at Billy. 'What kinda work?' he asked suspiciously.

'Catching horses,' Harry told him.

'Catching horses?' Billy echoed. 'We don't know nothing about that line of work.'

'That's a surprise,' Harry said, pulling his hat off again. 'What about it, Judge?'

'If you can pay their fines, they're yours,' Willet said, a little grudgingly.

Harry paid over the money and they walked out of the judge's house.

'You boy's got the price of a drink on you?' he asked.

'No, we ain't got the price of a drink on us,' Billy said.

'Then I guess I'd better go into one of the saloons for a bottle for tonight and a couple of bottles for the trail.' The boys waited while he got the whiskey.

'Got a place to stay?' he asked them.

'We had until Mister Slippery Fingers took our money,' Frank said.

'Then you boys can sleep in the livery with the horses and me. I don't see the old man objecting to you doin' that,' Harry said.

'Wal, if the horses don't object, I don't see how we can,' Billy laughed.

The old man was still awake when they got down there.

'Sure I don't mind you stayin',' he said. He gave the bottles that Harry was holding a knowing look.

Taking the hint, Harry asked the old man to get a mug. When he came back, Harry poured a generous measure of whiskey into it. Looking pleased, the old man scuttled away to drink it in a corner.

Harry and the boys took the rest of the bottle and went into a stall at the bottom of the stable. Pulling out the cork, Harry had a long drink and passed it to Billy, who after he had taken a long drink passed it to Frank.

'Is there much to this horse-catching business?' Billy asked, stretching out on a bale of hay.

'Not a damn thing,' Harry told him. 'You've just got to be smarter than them.' He grinned.

They spent an hour talking about horses and

horse catching. Gradually, under the effects of the whiskey Frank moved out into another stall and made himself a bed in the hay. Billy followed a few minutes later. Harry stayed up with the bottle for company, fighting off the black thoughts of his family, and what might have been. In the end he put the cork in the bottle and fell asleep.

Slim Loxton waited behind a rock, occasionally peeking out to look down the trail to see if he could see the Beaver stage. The trail was empty. He blew on his hands. Behind him Barney Webb, Jack Corey and Charlie Salmon waited in the trees for his signal. Loxton scowled and hurried over to them.

'OK,' Charlie,' he said. 'It's your turn. Get out there and keep them eyes peeled.' He blew on his hands again.

'Right, boss,' Salmon said as he went across to the boulder.

Charlie was getting to be a disappointed man. His old fella had ridden with Slim Loxton and his boys in the old days. His old man was a man he had never seen a lot of because he was either on the run, in jail, or getting better after collecting some lead. Being an outlaw wasn't half as glamorous as he had led his son to believe.

Charlie squinted and looked round. They'd tried building a fire under the trees. It hadn't worked. Even the boss couldn't get it going. The last job had gone wrong and they'd nearly ended up in jail. The food was always lousy, and when there was any money, there was no place to spend it. He pounded his arms across his chest to keep his circulation going.

Kate Battersby pushed herself up and tried to get comfortable. She pulled the blanket further round her that the stage driver had handed to her just before they pulled out of Lowry and headed up to Beaver.

She was glad of the warmth it provided her with, but she couldn't help wishing that she were back with her husband, Fred. She let go of the blanket to hold on to her hat that was slipping off her head. A wave of cold air pushed itself under the leather blind that kept most of the wind out. She took her hand away from her hat and pulled the blanket up again.

Up on the box it was worse. The freezing wind numbed the fingers of the driver, Jed Hallet. Its rawness cut through the fabric of his gloves like an Indian's scalping knife. Winding the leathers round his wrist, he slapped them against the team's backs and yelled at them. He knew that he couldn't take many more winters up on the box. Maybe it was time to find something else.

Bill Smithers pulled the buffalo robe more tightly round his body, and squinted into the thickening sleet. He sure as hell didn't like this job. He had done two runs. Jed was OK, but the weather was getting right into his bones. He shivered.

The minute they got into Beaver he was heading for a decent saloon, some decent drink and some decent whores. He'd drink his pay away and find some decent work. Maybe he'd go and see Fred Battersby. He had done some ranch work down on the plains and maybe Battersby would give him a job. A lot of his hands had picked up their pay and lit out when gold had been discovered. He reached inside his shirt and wrapped his numbed fingers round the half-bottle of whiskey. Pulling it out, he drew the cork with his teeth and took a long pull.

'Wanna finish it?' He handed it across to Jed.

Jed grinned and switched the leathers from one hand to the other.

'Thanks, *amigo*,' he grinned.

The whiskey burned fresh life into his body, and then he tossed it down on to the trail where it smashed against a rock.

'I can see 'em,' Charlie Salmon sang out.

He had been damn lucky to see them. A strong gust of wind had blown away the curtain of sleet giving him a glimpse of the coach and the team rounding the bend.

Loxton heard him first. 'OK, let's git.'

The others ran for their horses, and pulled at

the leathers that held them to a branch of a tree. Slim held Salmon's horse and handed him the leathers while he got into the saddle. He sure didn't look like his pa, but then his pa hadn't been home too much, so maybe Mrs Salmon had decided that she needed some company on the long dark nights when the gang was raising hell. Salmon snatched at the leathers and hauled himself into the saddle. They rode out on to the trail.

The warmth from the whiskey had burned into Bill's body and fingers. He saw the four figures. He poked Jed in the ribs and gestured in the direction of the men. Jed nodded vigorously and lashed the team. The team gave an extra hard tug on the reins.

Bill tried to pull the shotgun clear of the buffalo robes, but it snagged and the force of the movement nearly jerked it from his hands. The gun went off. Both barrels spat buckshot into the sleet.

Slim Loxton had his gun in his hand. He lined Bill up in the sights as the shotgun went off. He applied a mite more pressure to the trigger. The gun bucked and roared. Its slug spent itself between Bill's eyes. His hand reached for the rail, but he was already dead.

Jed had seen Bill die. A second later, he raised his hands to lash the team again, and drive through the four men, As he brought the leathers down on the backs of the team, a slug from Corey ploughed through his clothes and burst his heart. He screamed and died in the freezing mountain air.

Kate Battersby had heard the dull roar of the shotgun, and knew that something was wrong. She pulled back the leather blind just in time to see Jed fall from the box. Putting her hands to her mouth she stifled a scream, then braced herself against the side of the coach as it started to gather speed. Everything seemed to spin round her. Her head was continually banged against the leathers of the coach. The wheel hit a bump and her head smashed against the back of the seat so hard that she lost consciousness.

As she lost consciousness, the tongue holding the team snapped and they galloped off leaving the coach to carry her along the trail, its speed slowly decreasing, its wheels churning up the ground.

The four outlaws had scattered to the side of the trail as the coach ploughed through. Charlie Salmon was the first to recover from the surprise. Rowelling his horse, he hauled its head round and galloped after the coach. He wasn't too sure what he was going to do. He was saved from worrying too much about it as the coach slewed off the trail and came to a halt in the thick mud. The other three caught up with him and hauled their horses to a halt.

'OK Charlie, you get up an' throw that strong box down,' Slim Loxton called to him.

Charlie gigged his horse up against the side of the coach, got hold of the rail, and hauled himself up. On the roof, he headed for the footwell where the strong-box was kept. He looked into the footwell.

'Come on, kid,' Jack Corey shouted up. 'If you're much longer the posse'll be comin' up an' askin' us what we're doin'.'

'Give the kid a break,' Loxton said to him.

Corey glared at him and scrambled up on the top of the coach.

'Damn it,' he yelled. 'There ain't any strong-box up here.' He got down from the coach.

'You should see what's in here,' Barney Webb said, climbing out of the coach. He moved out of the way to let Loxton through. Loxton watched as Kate Battersby started to come round. Blood was running down the side of her face.

'Just the thing to keep us warm on a day like this,' Barney Webb said in a husky voice. 'Beats all the buffalo robes an' whiskey.'

Kate looked up with fear in her blue eyes. 'What do you want?' she groaned.

'We want the strong-box,' Loxton told her.

'Strong-box?' Kate asked groggily.

'Yeah, the strong-box,' Webb said to her. 'It's got the payroll for the Battersby ranch. It's gonna be a tidy haul.'

'My husband didn't send any money up with this stage this month. He was afraid the Loxton gang might try to steal it.'

Loxton narrowed his eyes at her. 'You Kate Battersby?' he asked.

'Yes,' she said, putting her hand to her head.

'It's plain nice to meet you Mrs Battersby,' Loxton told her. 'An' it's even nicer to know that the job ain't gonna be a complete waste of time. Git her outside,' Loxton said, jumping out of the stagecoach.

Webb grabbed the stunned woman and pulled her out into the sleet. She stood for a moment, her hand to her cut head, watching them as they crowded round her.

Jack Corey stood behind her, his eyes running dawn her slim figure.

'What are we gonna do with her, boss?' he asked.

'Not that,' Loxton told him. 'She's gonna make us some money.'

'How do you mean?' Barney Webb asked.

Loxton gave him a pained look. 'If the money ain't on the stage for us to take off it, then we're gonna have to ask her ol' man for it,' he said.

'My husband won't give you anything but a rope,' Kate Battersby snapped.

'Who the hell asked you?' Corey demanded, making to slap her.

Charlie Salmon took a step forward. He didn't

like the way things were shaping up. Webb had seen him, and not for the first time asked himself if the kid was up to the job. He let it ride.

'We'll just get her ol' man to do a swap. The money for his wife.' Loxton grinned wolfishly as he spoke. 'But whichever way we play it, all we're gonna get if we stand round here is pneumonia. Let's get back to the cabin an' dry out an' warm ourselves up with some whiskey.'

Harry and the boys rose early. They were getting their stuff together when the liveryman showed up.

'Sure did appreciate that whiskey last night,' he said. 'Maybe you'd like to share my coffee before you go?' He waved the pot at them.

'That'd be just fine,' Harry said. He had sent Frank out to Madam Reno's to get some sandwiches for their breakfast and some supplies for the trail.

While he was doing this he stood by the door of the livery watching the sleet. The sky was still heavy with clouds and the clouds were brimming with sleet. Billy came up with his and Frank's mug.

'Thought I heard something about coffee.'

'You heard right,' the liveryman told him.

The old man held the pot. Billy put the mug underneath it and waited. Harry watched as the thick black coffee struggled out of the pot and into the mug. A minute later Frank returned with a couple of packages. He tossed the smaller of them to Harry.

'Breakfast,' he said, putting the others in his saddle-bag with the supplies he had bought.

Harry ripped open the parcel and found half a dozen bacon sandwiches, still hot from the stove, with butter dripping down over the bread. After he had passed them round he gave one to the old man.

'That's fine,' the old man said, biting into the bread.

They ate the sandwiches and drank the coffee in silence. When they had finished up, Harry settled the bill with the liveryman and got the gear together. They led the horses outside and mounted up. Harry tipped his hat to the livery-man and they set out. As they passed the sheriff's office, Harry saw the sheriff and one of his deputies holding a couple of horses. 'Better get a posse up and find out what happened.'

'Best tell Fred Battersby,' Mitch said.

Brad gave him a questioning look.

'Kate Battersby was on that stage. Fred's gonna be none too pleased if anythin's happened to her.'

'The wife of the biggest rancher in the territory in an accident; that's just what I need at election time,' the sheriff said.

'What's goin' on here?' Fred Battersby asked, watching the expressions on the faces of the men.

Bracing himself, the sheriff looked him in the eye. 'The team that was haulin' the stage just came gallopin' into town, with no stage.'

Fred watched the man's face. 'Well, we'd best get a posse out to find it.'

'We're doin' that Fred,' Brad told him. 'Mitch, start rounding up some men.'

'What else are you going to do about it?' Fred demanded impatiently.

'Simmer down, Fred. I know Kate's on the stage, but there's no sense in going off half-cocked. We'd be doing more harm than good, especially in this kind of weather.'

'Don't tell me we'd be doing more harm than good,' Fred blazed up.

'OK. We've got to get a posse together, then we can start backtracking them,' Brad said reasonably. He had plenty experience of Fred's temper, and found that Fred talked first, and then thought about it.

'I'm holding you personally responsible if anythin' happens to Kate!' Fred shouted.

A crowd had started to gather round the argument. Fred looked them over. 'If any of you boys want to make some extra money, just you sign up for this posse. I'll foot the bill,' he called over to them.

Brad caught his sleeve. 'That ain't the best idea in the world,' he said.

'Why would that be?' Fred demanded.

'Come across to my office. We can talk there,' Brad said.

They crossed the street with the sleet fading out, leaving the sky an iron grey.

As they did so, three horsemen guided their horses round them.

'Somebody looks like he lost a dollar and found a cent,' Harry said.

Frank, who was leading the packhorse they had purchased, gave him a smile.

'He sure does, doesn't he? The sheriff's not looking too happy either. Maybe Judge Willet hasn't given him his share of the fine money yet.'

Brad led Fred into the office. 'Fred, you can't go round hirin' whoever you want for this kinda job. We'll end up gettin' in each other's way and maybe end up shooting each other.'

'It's my money and I'll do what I want with it,' came the angry answer from Fred. 'Especially if it helps Kate.'

It was Brad's turn to get real angry. 'You know damn well it ain't just a question of money. Like you said, especially if it's a question of helping Kate. Have you taken a good look at them men out there? Barflies, loafers. Men who wouldn't know a day's work if it got up and bit them. We don't need that kind of man. We need men who'll stick at it. Men who can use a gun. Not men who'll come running home when it starts snowing again.'

Fred had fallen silent, like he had just had the wind taken out of his sails. He looked out of the window for a moment at the sky.

'I guess you're right Brad, but I want Kate home safe and sound. If anythin' goes wrong and I think it's your fault, I'll kill you.'

Brad could see that he meant it. 'OK,' he said.

FOUR

Kate Battersby's head was still aching as the gang hauled the horses to a halt outside the cabin. Her head ached and her wrists burned under the pressure of the ropes that Loxton had tied them with. They ached from her continuous efforts to get them off, but Loxton had done his job well. After a while, she gave it up. The last thing she wanted was to have him tie her even tighter. If he looked at them and realized she had been trying to get loose, she didn't know what he'd do.

Barney Webb dragged her none too gently off one of the horses from the stage they had managed to catch. Loxton opened the door. He pushed her inside the cabin. The place smelled foul.

'Shall I untie her?' Corey asked, looking her up and down as he had done when they had found her in the stage.

Loxton nodded. 'Sure. Charlie, you keep an eye

on her. See she doesn't go wanderin' off.'

'Right, boss,' Charlie replied.

'Barney get them horses unsaddled and feed them,' Loxton said, taking a bottle of whiskey out of the cupboard and pouring some drinks. He handed them round and raised his glass in salute.

'Here's to pay day,' he said.

'Pay day?' Kate Battersby asked, rubbing her wrists. 'The only thing my husband will pay you with is a bullet or a rope.'

Loxton turned on her. Charlie Salmon saw the look in his eyes. Loxton stopped suddenly, and poured himself another drink.

'Get the fire going, kid. We don't want Mrs Battersby catching cold up here in this fresh mountain air.' He laughed.

Charlie went out to the back of the cabin to where the woodpile was and picked up an armful from under the tarpaulin. Inside, he laid it among the cold ashes of the previous day's fire. He scraped a match along the stones, and cupped the flame in his hand. He let it grow for a few seconds, then put it among the shards of wood and let it burn. After a minute or so he put in a second match.

Kate Battersby was leaning against the table with her arms round her chest, shivering. Charlie tossed her a blanket off his bed.

'Hold this round you. It ain't much, but it'll help,' he said.

'Wal, ain't that sweet?' Corey said, from the corner where he nursed a whiskey.

'Hell, she's old enough to be my ma.' Charlie laughed uncomfortably. Kate watched him.

A plan was starting to form in her mind. 'That's very kind of you,' she said, as sweetly as she could, and gave Charlie a smile that was less than motherly.

Loxton watched her intently as she spoke. Maybe she wasn't so dumb after all, 'Git some grub fer us, Charlie, and make sure you put enough out for Mrs Battersby. Do you mind if I call you Kate?' he said sarcastically.

Her tongue thickened in her mouth as she cut off a reply.

Charlie rooted among the provisions in the cabin. There was bacon, beans and some bread. He put the grub out on the stove and started it cooking.

'Best fix some coffee as well,' Corey called to him. 'I can't see our guest likin' whiskey overmuch.'

Behind his back Salmon tossed him a hard look. Kate shivered and walked across to the fire. She spread her hands out in front of it. The heat smoothed out her wrinkled skin. She massaged them, trying to get the circulation going again. All the time Corey watched her movements as he sipped at his whiskey.

Night was starting to fall as Harry and the others reached sheltered ground near some trees. The trees held the wind off them.

'We'll call it a day here,' he said to them as he pulled on the leathers to halt his horse.

The boys didn't need much telling to get things moving. They hobbled the horses and got the food unpacked. Then Harry started to get it ready. The food and the whiskey cheered them. After a while they turned in.

'What's that?' Frank asked, his hands reaching for his gun.

'It ain't nothin' to be scared of,' Harry said, with a smile. 'Just a plain ol' timber wolf. The fire'll keep it away.'

Frank turned and looked in the direction of the trees, a shudder running through his body. Billy grinned. Frank pulled himself closer to the fire.

'How long will it be before we catch sight of them horses?'

Harry made to face the fire. 'A spell. We've got to get down the other side of this mountain. The weather's got to clear up.'

A wolf howled again.

'It might be harder this year. Spring's gonna be late.'

'How late?' Billy asked.

'I ain't rightly sure,' Harry said.

They talked for a while longer, then the boys slept. Harry listened to the wolf for a while.

*

Brad whittled the posse down to a manageable handful of men. They found the stage where Loxton and his gang had left it. The tongue was broken, the wheels were up to their hubs in mud, and the two bodies were half a mile down the trail.

'There's no need to ask where Kate is,' Fred said angrily.

'No, they've taken her with them,' Brad said after he had examined the hoof prints in the mud.

He could see that Fred was practically breathing fire. He was twisting the leathers round his fingers.

'Let's find the trail,' Fred said suddenly.

'OK,' Brad said to the others. He caught Mitch's arm.

'Keep an eye on Fred,' he said to his deputy.

'I have been doing,' was the reply.

They got into the saddles and started to follow the trail. The snow had stopped falling and the ground was beginning to freeze.

'They're headed up this way,' Brad told Fred, as he pulled up level with the rancher.

Brad squinted at the jagged peaks far ahead. He did not want to be the one to tell Fred that there were any number of canyons leading up into the mountains, and all of them would be equally hard-going. He wondered how long the posse would keep moving. There hadn't been a lot of time to collect supplies. They had enough for a day or two. Three at most. Then they'd have to be thinking of turning for home. Brad blamed himself for it. He should have been a damn sight more forceful with Fred and waited for them to collect more supplies. They rode on across the open ground, breaking the thin layers of ice forming over the water beneath.

They went on for an hour or so in silence with Brad continually watching the light fade. He was putting off the moment when he would have to tell Fred that he was calling a halt for the day. Finally, the moment came just as the blood-red streaks were falling across the sky.

Brad threw up his hand. 'All right, this is it Fred. We can't go any further. There ain't enough light for us to see the trail. We're only gonna miss it in the dark.'

He felt Fred's glare as Fred looked across at him. 'I say there's enough time left yet to make up a few more miles on them.'

'And what if we miss them? What then, Fred?' It was Brad's turn to twist the leathers round his knuckles.

'Just what is the matter with you, Brad? Are you scared of the dark?' Fred's voice was full of childish petulance.

Brad felt himself colour up. He knew that it was a stupid thing to do. His anger started to rise. He gulped it back down his throat. He wanted to pull Fred out of the saddle and give him a beating, but he knew that he wouldn't do that. Then Fred backed down.

'All right, this is it for today,' Fred said, and dismounted.

It took them a long time to build a fire. While they were doing it, Brad realized that the day after tomorrow they would have to think about turning back, unless they caught up with the outlaws. They slept uneasily, with their heads on their saddles and their thin saddle-blankets over them.

Kate Battersby also slept uneasily, surrounded by the three badmen. She did not count Charlie Salmon, who was hardly more than a boy. She moved restlessly, pulling the blankets more tightly round her. The embers of the fire fell lower and lower, until they caved in on themselves, sending up a shower of sparks. By the brief flare of the dying flames, she could make out the men. They all seemed to be asleep except Charlie Salmon, who was tossing and turning restlessly.

She had pegged him from early on. If anybody was going to help her out of this mess, it was Charlie Salmon. It wouldn't take much to talk him round, she thought. She turned over and fell asleep, feeling cold and hungry.

'So how do you reckon you're gonna work this with Fred Battersby?'

It was the following morning and Slim Loxton, Barney Webb and Jack Corey were standing in the weak sunlight outside the cabin.

'We're gonna send young Charlie down with a note for Battersby. We're gonna tell him we want two thousand dollars or we'll send his wife back in little pieces. That should do it.'

Jack Corey scratched the greying stubble on his chin, 'You reckon we should trust Charlie? He don't seem to be going wholeheartedly for this scheme.'

'We haven't any choice, besides, if Fred Battersby does do somethin' stupid, like hanging the kid, it ain't any great loss. We've still got his woman,' Loxton told him.

Corey ruminated for a moment, then said, 'I don't like it.'

'You got a better idea?' Barney Webb asked him. 'Because if you ain't, I have.'

'Let's hear it,' Loxton said, resting his foot on a bar of the old corral.

'We'd get a good price for her up in Shacktown,' he said slowly.

'Shacktown?' Loxton repeated slowly. 'It's a good ride from here, an' all up into the mountains. There's no tellin' what kinda reception we'd get there.'

'They'd pay us, an' they know us. They're always short of female flesh up there,' Corey cut in quickly.

42

It seemed a better idea than risking a bullet from Fred Battersby, and there was the posse to consider. There was sure to be one after them by now.

They sat in silence for a moment, then Loxton said, 'We'll see how it goes with Battersby first, and if it doesn't work out we'll go to Shacktown.'

Having seen the three men go outside, Kate Battersby guessed that they were up to something. Now she was going to have to think hard about getting Charlie Salmon to help her. Salmon was out at the back cutting more wood for the fire. She'd make a start on him today, she decided.

Loxton came in and poured himself a whiskey. She watched him for a moment, then she went to the door.

'Where do you think you're goin?' he demanded harshly.

'Just to get some fresh air. This place ain't exactly brand-new-spanking clean is it?' she asked angrily.

For a moment, he stood and looked at her, as if trying to decide what she meant. In the end he just grunted and said, 'Don't go too far or the boys might get the wrong idea.'

Kate opened the door and went outside. She pulled the blanket more tightly round her. Beneath the blanket she wore a coat, the one she had bought in Lowry before getting the stage for home. She had lost the matching gloves some place.

The mud pulled at her heels and she had trouble getting round to where Salmon was cutting the wood. He wore a thick sheepskin jacket and a hat with his bandanna tied over it so that the wind couldn't blow it away. She watched the axe rise and fall. Its blade sank into the wood, sending up a heap of splinters. For a moment Salmon was unaware of her presence, then he seemed to sense her. He stopped chopping at the wood and turned round. His face was red and sweaty with the effort.

'Hi,' she said coyly.

A self-conscious smile broke out on Salmon's face.

'Hi,' he returned, laying the axe down.

'I heard you cutting wood and wondered if you needed some company?' she said with a smile.

'I'd sure appreciate it. It's not that me an' the other boys don't get on, but we ain't got all that much in common,' he told her.

'No, I can see that,' she said, giving him a speculative look.

They talked for a few minutes, but then Corey came out to look for her.

'It was gettin' kinda quiet out here,' he told them. 'I thought I'd best come and see what was goin' on.'

'Nothing's going on,' Kate said quickly. 'I was just giving Charlie some company.'

'As long as that's all you're givin' him,' Corey spoke coarsely.

Charlie coloured up. 'There ain't no call for that kinda talk,' he said.

Corey looked him up and down. 'If you figure you can do anythin' about it,' he said, 'I'd be more than willin' to oblige you.'

As he spoke Webb came from round the back. 'How's that wood chopping comin' along? We're gonna be plumb froze to death if you don't get a move on, Charlie.'

'I was just bringin' a pile in,' Salmon told him, dropping the axe at Corey's feet. He picked up the wood he had cut.

Inside the cabin, the four men pulled out a deck of dog-eared playing cards and started to play poker for matches. Kate sat in a corner trying to get warm. Corey's voice had told her that she was going to have to move quickly, or he might just gun Charlie Salmon down.

After an hour the men were bored and had thrown the cards in a heap in the middle of the table. Kate watched them as she tried to find a reason for getting outside with Salmon. Nothing seemed to present itself until Loxton suddenly said, 'Charlie go an' check the horses.'

'Yeah. Sure,' he said.

Kate saw her opportunity. 'I've got to get out as well. I haven't had any fresh air since this morning. This is killing me.'

Slim Loxton gave her a wary look. 'Don't be out there all night, that's all.'

'OK,' she said and went outside.

Salmon led her round to the lean-to that the

gang had built to give the horses some shelter.

Kate spoke desperately and urgently. 'You haven't a chance of getting a cent for me. Fred would sooner let them keep me rather than hand over a cent,' she lied.

'I don't figure on that being the whole truth,' Salmon told her. 'I ain't all that sure they'd let you go if he did pay up.' He ran his hand over his horse's flanks as he spoke. The animal skittered a little nervously, then settled down.

'You really mean they'd kill me?' Kate asked with genuine fear.

'Yeah. There isn't anything any of us have got to lose.' He fed his horse a handful of hay.

'Even you?' she asked.

'I don't know,' he said hesitatingly.

'Will you help me get away?' she asked him.

'Sure I'll help you get back to Beaver and your husband,' he said huskily.

'That's wonderful,' Kate reached up and kissed him.

'It's got to be tonight though,' he told her. 'Slim's gonna send me down with a ransom note tomorrow.'

Kate looked at him. 'Tonight?'

'Tonight.'

'We'd better be making a start,' she said.

'I already have. I figured you'd ask me. I've stuck some extra grub in the lean-to. We should have enough. I don't know what we're gonna run into down there.' He indicated the valley below.

Kate gave him a worried look, 'You'd better be sure about this,' she said. 'If this goes wrong before we can get out of here, they'll kill us both.'

'Yeah, I know,' Charlie told her. 'We'd better get inside.'

Kate turned and went round the cabin to the front.

'I was just comin' to look fer you,' Corey said with a grin. 'I was beginning to wonder what was keepin' you an' yer beau.'

The colour left Kate's face. She licked her lips. 'The air's fresher out here than in there,' she said, attempting to push past him, but Corey caught her arm and held it tight, his fingers going white as he gripped her. Kate stiffened, and tried to pull her arm away.

Corey smiled down at her. 'I wish you was mine,' he told her, pushing her into the cabin. 'It'd be a real pleasure showing you who was boss.'

She went into the cabin. Loxton was lying on his bunk, his hands folded under his head. Barney Webb was sitting at the table playing with the cards and taking no notice of anybody.

Time crawled by for Kate Battersby. She was literally counting the seconds before they all turned in and Charlie Salmon came to take her to the horses. Corey served up the grub at chow time. Beans, bacon and coffee. She almost turned up her nose at it, but she knew she was going to need her strength for her escape.

47

'Not to your liking?' Corey asked suddenly.

Kate looked up at him and bit off an answer. 'No, it's fine,' she said.

'Well, your face don't say it's fine,' Corey said to her, and walked across the cabin, then sat down with Webb.

Kate felt him looking at her as they ate. She wondered if he suspected what was going to happen. She pushed the thought aside and ate as much of the food as she could stomach. Salmon came across with some more coffee for her. The night wore on, and one by one they turned in. Loxton went last.

Kate lay on her bed listening to the regular breathing of the men. After about an hour or so, she heard the floorboards creak and the approach of footsteps. A hand was clamped over her mouth, and Salmon whispered, 'Are you ready?'

She nodded her head. He moved his hand and crept away from the bed. Her eyes accustomed to the dark, Kate could make out the outline of his body. The snoring of the other three was the only sound in the cabin. When they got outside, the cold night air hit her and she gasped at the shock of it.

'Follow me,' Salmon whispered. The wind whistled through the lean-to.

Salmon lit a lamp, saddled up two of the horses and put the leathers on them. They led the horses out of the lean-to, and walked down as far as the trail.

'No point in chargin' out of here,' Salmon said to
her. 'Especially if nobody's listening.' He gave a
nervous laugh.

The chill wind crawled through Kate's skin and
into her bones. It stung her eyes and made them
water. Her lips were chapped and sore.

'It's just so damn cold.' She pulled the coat
further round her.

'Don't worry,' he told her. 'You'll soon be home.'

Kate hoped that she would.

Harry woke stiff and cold. He looked round. He
could not see Billy or Frank. He got up from under
the blankets. Then he saw Frank, who was bent
over the embers of the fire trying to get them
burning again. The flames suddenly came to life,
licking at the surrounding wood. Frank gathered
up a couple more logs and fed them to the blaze.

'Want some coffee?' he called to Harry.

'Sure, if there's any goin',' Harry said, making
his way to the fire. 'Where's Billy?'

'Billy's down there catching breakfast,' Frank
said, passing a mug to Harry.

Harry wrapped his hands round it and looked
across the trail. He could see the water of the
stream glistening in the sunshine. He caught the
sudden movement among the trees. He focused
his eyes so that he could make out Billy casting
his rod into the water.

'It shouldn't be too long,' Frank said. 'Billy can't do much, but he can fish.'

Harry tipped a measure of whiskey into his mug, and let it warm his bones. Going back to where he had left his pack, he found his .45. It had been a long time since he had last used it, but a cold feeling had come over him, and it was not the weather. The clearing they had camped in was peaceful. Standing up, he watched Billy starting towards the camp waving a line with some fish on it. Harry grinned to himself. He was sure glad that he had met up with the youngsters. He walked to meet the boy.

'Got three big ones for you here,' Billy called out. 'The stream's full of them. They're waiting to be caught,' he said, putting the fish down for Frank to clean.

Harry emptied his mug, and poured some coffee for Billy. Frank picked up the fish and slit them so that he could clean them.

'I'll get some sticks to put them on, so they can cook,' Harry said, walking up the trail to look for sticks. They weren't so easy to find as he thought they might be.

He reached a thick piece of foliage when he heard the horses galloping towards him. At first he saw nothing, then two horses burst through the foliage. Throwing himself to one side, Harry hit the thicket and turned in time to see a man and woman rowelling their horses down the trail.

Getting to his feet, Harry cursed. Picking up his hat, he slapped it against his side and looked after them, but they had already disappeared, leaving a trail of broken undergrowth behind them.

Quickly, he ran down to the camp. Everything seemed all right there, but Frank and Billy were standing round looking dazed.

'What do you reckon that was?' Frank asked.

'I ain't rightly sure, but I didn't like the look or sound of it,' Harry told him.

A few yards away his rifle lay in his saddle holster.

'You boys got one of these?' he said pointing to his Winchester. 'If you have you'd better git hold of it.'

'We ain't got nothin' like that, jest a couple of old hand guns,' Billy said. 'Why, you expectin' trouble?'

'I wouldn't be askin' if I wasn't,' Harry said, stepping across to get his rifle and check that it was loaded.

Charlie Salmon was in the lead. He had hauled on the leathers of his horse to slow it down, now that the trail was getting both steep and rocky. Occasionally, the moon uncovered and the way ahead was lit for a spell, but then it got dark again and the doubt returned to Charlie's mind. The long, overhanging branches plucked at the faces of the two riders, and once Kate cried out in surprise and pain. Salmon hauled his horse to a halt and went back to see what the matter was. He found Kate holding her face. He felt the warm blood running down it.

'How is it?' he asked, anxiously. He threw a look down the back trail.

'It's nothing,' Kate assured him, wiping the blood off her face with her hand. 'Let's get going. They can't be far behind now.'

'No,' Salmon said. 'They can't.' His voice sounded nervous and edgy in the dark.

Kate felt his nervousness, and started to feel afraid once more. She had seen how the others acted, and Charlie Salmon wasn't in their league.

Kate gigged her horse and followed Salmon along the trail. Beside the trail there was a long drop. Below, she could hear the river in full flood after the snow. It roared down the valley. She shuddered. If her horse missed its footing, there wouldn't be any hope for her. She tried to focus on the rear of Salmon's, with its white tail, but she was tired and her eyes had trouble staying open. She shivered again and wrapped the leathers even more tightly round her frozen fingers. Squinting, she watched the rear of Salmon's horse.

Salmon turned in his saddle and looked in Kate's direction. The trail was narrower than he remembered. The long drop made him sweat. The rising wind spooked the horses. He suddenly felt the need for a shot of whiskey. He licked his lips. Salmon looked up to the east. The first hints of day were appearing in the sky. It would be another day and a half before they got to Beaver. A day and a half at least.

'I'll be damn glad when the sun comes up,' Webb said, straining to see any tracks in the dark. If Salmon had any savvy, which Webb reckoned he didn't, he could have made things real hard with a couple of rifle shots thrown down at them from the cover of the trees. Webb looked up. He was having the same trouble that Kate Battersby was having. It was dark and his eyes were tired, and the trail was dangerous.

'Hey, boss,' Webb called out.

'Yeah,' Loxton hauled on the leathers of his horse and pulled it to a halt. The animals skidded a mite and canted in the direction of the trail's edge. His hand tightened on the leathers and an oath froze in his throat.

'Why don't we call a halt an' push on when the light's better in the mornin'? We can't see a damn thing this way,' Webb called over Corey's head. Corey was in the middle of the party.

For a moment Loxton thought about it. 'No, we'll go on. If they pull off the trail we might miss them.' Corey said nothing. It hadn't seemed a bad idea at the time, but Loxton was the boss. He shivered. When they caught up with Salmon, he was going to get a bullet between the eyes, and when they caught up with Kate Battersby, he was going to make sure she warmed up to him a mite.

Like Salmon and Kate Battersby, they moved on watching it slowly get lighter and lighter.

Loxton's hand fell to his gun, and he let out a yell. 'They're there.'

Then he rowelled his horse and galloped on.

Kate Battersby heard the shout. She suddenly felt sick, and forced herself to turn round. She saw Loxton, gun in hand, riding hell for leather down the trail. Salmon also turned, his gun in his hand, fear in his heart.

'Come on,' he yelled, moving to one side of the trail, so as to allow Kate to pass him. When she had done, he pulled his horse's head round and went after her, tossing a shot at Loxton.

Loxton did not even feel the wind of the shot, but he rowelled his horse savagely. Kate's horse just missed Harry, forcing him to dive into the undergrowth. Salmon followed a minute later. Loxton, Corey and Webb tore down the trail, their faces white with anger.

Harry had just finished speaking to the boys and had gone to get his rifle. The three men were firing wildly as they rode through. One bullet struck Billy in the side of the head. Frank fell with one in his heart.

For a moment the world stopped for Harry. Levering a shell into the breech, he threw a hopeless shot after the trio. As the sound of the hoof beats died away, he ran over to where the two boys lay, their blood running into the ground. It was his family all over again. The nightmare was revisiting him.

He stood in the middle of the trail, a great emptiness filling his heart. His mouth hung open in despair. Now, he would never show them how to catch horses and break them like he had been going to show his own boy.

The weak sun faded away leaving the sky black and empty. A wind started to get up. Harry pulled his sheepskin jacket more tightly round his body. His years suddenly seemed to catch up with him, and he felt himself buckle under their weight. He wanted to cry and rage at heaven. In the end, he just got a shovel from the pack and buried them. When he had finished he fixed up two crosses and stuck them in the ground before saying a few words.

The world seemed empty of everything after he had put the boys under. He stood around wondering what to do next. He forced himself to pick up the stuff that made up their camp. There was little enough of it, but he gathered it up and fixed it into some parcels, and put it over the back of the spare horse. The three fish that Billy had caught a few hours ago lay rotting on the ground. Harry picked them up and threw them into the undergrowth.

His mind turned to the riders who had shot down the boys. Where were they going? Why were they chasing the other two riders? He was sure that was what they were doing. Almost painfully, he got into the saddle of his own horse and rode down the trail holding the leathers of the other horses. It was easy to pick out the trail of the riders. He just kept following it down the mountain through the smashed undergrowth.

'You can go back to Beaver if you want, Brad.' Fred Battersby's voice was high and angry. 'But don't look for my support when the election comes up.'

'I wasn't going to anyway,' Brad shouted at him. He was starting to get angry now. 'Can't you see we ain't prepared for a long chase in this weather or in this country?' Brad told him.

'Then what are you prepared for?' Fred bit out. 'Just some jaunt to make it look good? That's my wife those bastards have got.'

'I know that Fred,' Brad tried again. 'If we go up there like this, we're going to come back with our tails between our legs.'

Fred glowered at him, then said, 'Me an' these boys are going on until we catch up with them.'

Fred rowelled his horse and headed out, followed by half a dozen men who had agreed to go along with him. Brad watched them go, knowing that no good would come of it.

'Gather round,' he said to the remainder of the posse. They formed a semi-circle round him. 'We're going to go back for the time being. It's like

I told Fred, we need more supplies if we're going to go up there,' he said, pointing to the mountain tops. 'An' even then it isn't goin' to be easy.' The rest of the posse growled its agreement.

Charlie Salmon was still out in front, and he was real scared. He could hear Loxton and the others catching up, and catching up fast. He threw a look over his shoulder. Kate had fallen back on him a mite. She was hanging on to the leathers and was bent low over the horse's neck. From what he could see her face was white and drawn.

'You've got to move faster,' he yelled, and waved his hand.

'I'm tryin' to,' the white-faced woman cried out. 'There's something wrong with my saddle. It's loose.'

Charlie swore. He got back to her and leaned down and inspected the saddlework. It was on the point of snapping. They were in a hell of a mess.

He leaned over. 'You're gonna have to ride with me,' he said, sweeping her up and swinging her up behind him. Kate squealed. Salmon rowelled his horse and urged it on.

'I can see 'em,' Corey yelled. The three men had stopped to give their horses a breather. Corey was on top of a rock. It gave him a good view of the land below.

Loxton scrambled up behind him and looked in the direction Corey was pointing. 'You're damn right,' he said, then jumped down.

Corey followed him to where Webb was holding the horses. They told him what they had seen and set off after the fugitives. It did not take their horses long to eat up the ground.

Loxton drew his gun when Kate came into sight round a bend in the trail. She looked round and pounded Salmon on the shoulder when she saw them. Salmon turned and saw the three riders bearing down on them, and as he did so, Loxton threw out a shot. Salmon's horse stumbled, and Salmon and Kate were thrown clear of the falling horse. Drawing his gun, Salmon scrambled to his feet, followed by Kate.

Salmon got into the cover of some boulders and started to trade shots with Loxton and his boys. Kate was holding her hands to her head and fighting back the tears.

'Why the hell did I let you talk me into this?' she yelled at him. 'Fred would have paid the ransom and I could have gone home.' She was nearly hysterical.

Salmon looked at her. 'You should have said that before you agreed to come with me.' Then he tossed a shot in Loxton's direction.

'Come out, Salmon. Just hand her over to us and you can walk away from this!' Loxton yelled.

'Like hell, I can,' Salmon called back.

A couple more shots rang out. The lead flew over Salmon's head.

Some distance away, Fred Battersby threw up his hand and halted the men behind him.

'I can hear shooting,' Fred shouted. 'Follow me. It's got to be them.'

They all drew their guns and followed Fred's lead. Fred galloped down the trail and into the clearing. Kate saw them coming and recognized him.

'Over here, Fred,' she yelled and stood up.

Salmon caught her by the waist and pulled her down, out of the line of fire.

'Kate,' Fred yelled, oblivious to the firing going on around him. He jumped out of the saddle, firing as he ran.

Jack Corey saw the running figure. Levelling his gun at him, he lined Fred up in his sights and squeezed the trigger. The slug tore into Fred, lifting him off his feet and throwing him down on the ground. Kate saw him fall.

'Fred!' she screamed and jumped to her feet.

The others behind Fred Battersby watched him fall. Up to that minute, they had followed him, but now that he had taken a bullet they weren't so sure. As one man, they turned their horses and galloped away.

Kate ran across the ground to where her husband had fallen. His face was white and lifeless. A great crimson stain was spreading over his shirt. Loxton, Corey, and Webb seized their opportunity and tore into the cover where a scared Charlie Salmon crouched.

'Hi, Charlie,' Loxton said, kicking his gun out of his hand.

Salmon looked up at him, his hands trembling.

'Get on yer feet,' Loxton told him. Grabbing him by the sleeve, he dragged Salmon over to where Kate was crouching over her husband. She was trying to cradle his head in her hands. Webb pulled her away from the body.

'I guess we could take a vote on it,' Loxton laughed sarcastically. 'On the other hand, we might as well save ourselves the trouble.' He flicked his wrist and put two bullets into Salmon's hide. Salmon twisted away, his face creased in his dying agony. His legs buckled and he fell.

'Put her on a horse,' Loxton said to Webb.

Dragging her to her feet, Webb pushed Kate in the direction of Salmon's horse. Her crying and screechings were echoing through the clearing. Roughly, he pushed her into the saddle.

'You stay up there, and don't do anything stupid,' he told her.

Kate looked down at him through the tears. She tried to kick at him, but Webb caught her foot.

'Try that agin an' you'll end up on the floor,' he said.

The others mounted up, and they headed in the direction of the cabin.

FIVE

They just missed colliding with Harry. Harry had turned off the main trail and taken a less well-marked trail to the left. He wanted some time to pull himself together. Hitching his horse to tree, he got a small fire going and made himself some coffee. Hunkering down by the fire, he sipped at the coffee and thought about what to do next. After a while, he threw the slops on to the fire and stood up. The best thing he could do would be to go to Beaver and see if he could get some help from there.

As he rode on, crossing Loxton's trail, he saw Charlie Salmon's body, before he saw Fred Battersby lying in a pool of blood.

'You've bin damn lucky,' he told Fred. 'Reckon it's missed your heart by a hair's-breadth.'

Fred's eyes flickered and he looked up at Harry. 'They've got Kate,' he gasped.

'She yer wife?' Harry asked him as he cleaned the wound out.

'Yeah,' Fred said, with difficulty. Then he told Harry all about it.

'I'll get you down to Beaver,' Harry said, struggling to lift Fred. He got him into the saddle and started down to Beaver.

Brad took the news of Fred's return with a feeling of relief.

'Can't tell you who the other fella was,' Brad said standing at his desk filling up two mugs of coffee for him and Harry.

'Maybe he was one of the gang,' Harry said helpfully.

'Maybe. What are your plans now?' he asked the horse trader.

Harry looked speculatively into his mug for a moment, then he said, 'I don't rightly know fer sure. I guess you're goin' up after this fella Loxton.'

'It's a big place up there an' he's gonna take some finding. They've probably killed Kate Battersby by now. I'm not sure it would do much good.'

This took Harry by surprise and made him angry. 'What about Billy and Frank?' he asked. 'Don't they deserve something?'

Brad looked away. 'Yeah, they deserve something, but I ain't got the men to go after them.'

Harry had not known Kate Battersby, but he had come to know the boys and they deserved something.

'All right, I'll find them myself,' he said.

Brad looked at him sharply. 'You won't stand a chance, but if you find them, you be sure you bring them back in one piece.'

'It'll be hard, but I'll try,' Harry told him as he left the office.

'What are we goin' to do with her now?' Barney Webb asked nobody in particular as he tipped some more whiskey into his mug.

Kate Battersby lay on a bunk. She was still in a daze from what had happened, especially the shooting of Fred. Her eyes were open and staring, as she looked up at the ceiling.

'I could think of a lot of things,' Corey said, his eyes skimming over her.

'No, you can't,' Loxton said quickly. 'We've lost enough money on this deal up to now. No greenbacks from the stage. Now we're stuck with her,' he said, jabbing a finger in Kate's direction.

'You sound as though you've got something in mind,' Corey snarled at him.

Loxton said nothing for a minute. 'Like I was sayin', they're always lookin' for new females in Shacktown.'

Webb sat up as if he had been hit with a red-hot iron. 'Yeah, like I said, they always want new females up there.' He laughed. 'They'll pay top dollar for her.'

Kate's head moved slowly round. She opened

her mouth to speak, but words failed her. She wanted to know where Shacktown was.

'You'll love it up there, honey,' Loxton shouted across to her, seeing her expression. 'You'll meet some real interestin' people.'

'A heap of real interestin' men you mean,' Corey guffawed loudly.

Kate pushed herself up on one elbow wondering what on earth they were talking about.

'You get a good night's sleep, honey,' Webb called out. 'You're gonna need all your strength.'

She turned to the wall and tried to sleep. She didn't know what Shacktown was or where it was, but she didn't like the sound of it. After a while she drifted off into a nightmare-haunted sleep.

She could see Fred hitting the ground, blood spurting from his shirt, the colour draining from his face. She saw the face of Charlie Salmon, white with terror, as Loxton passed sentence and executed him with his six-gun. Finally, she slept without memories or nightmares. It did not last long. Soon she felt Loxton's hand on her shoulder, shaking her awake.

His unshaven face grinned down at her. 'Your turn to do the cookin', Mrs Battersby.' He put his hand under her shoulder and pulled her out of the bunk.

'One thing I'll miss about young Charlie is his cookin',' he laughed. 'Yeah. The grub's in the kitchen there. There ain't much of it, but you can do somethin' with it.'

'I need a wash first,' Kate told him.

'You do some cookin' first then you can wash,' Loxton told her, grabbing her arm and pushing her towards the kitchen.

Barney Webb sat up on his bunk, grinning at what was going on. 'You tell her, boss.'

Kate went into the kitchen massaging her arm as she went. Near a set of drawers she found some bacon and a couple of tins of beans, along with some coffee.

'I'm going to have to go outside for some water, unless one of you would like to do it,' she said.

'Barney, you go with her. Make sure she doesn't get up to any mischief,' Loxton said.

Webb got out of his bed, and followed Kate outside. She hunkered down with the kettle beside the stream. Webb took a leak by the side of the cabin. He came back fastening up his trouser buttons.

'You got all you want?' he asked her as she put the lid back on the kettle.

'It's full,' she said pointing to the kettle.

'Back inside,' Webb told her.

Kate went inside the cabin and started to boil the kettle. While she was waiting for it, she made a start on the bacon and beans. The smell of the cooking helped mask some of the other smells. Occasionally, one of the outlaws looked in on her.

When the meal was cooked, she set it out on greasy plates and took it in to them.

'Smells pretty good,' Corey said, taking the plate from her.

Kate moved quickly to one side, having noticed his hand moving in the direction of her skirts. Barney Webb tittered. Loxton said nothing. She brought her own food and coffee into the room and sat on the edge of a bunk. She watched them eat.

The horse trader slept better than he might have thought when he settled down in the bed at the Lucky Strike hotel. The place still smelled of paint and freshly-cut timber.

The night before, he had decided on paying out for a decent bed in the hotel. He had gone to bed early, not wishing to try his luck at the tables. He had eaten at Madam Reno's and gone over to the hotel. After he had checked in, he went straight up to his room. At first, he found it difficult to sleep with the noise from the saloon and gambling halls along the street but, eventually, he made it.

At daybreak, he went across to Madam Reno's for some breakfast. After he had eaten, he returned to the hotel and checked his money. He walked along to the livery. While he was there, he sold the spare horses, except one, to the livery-man.

He headed out of town. As he rode down the street, the batwings of a saloon burst open, and he recognized Mr Slippery Fingers, being frog-marched out by four burly miners.

Harry gigged his horse to avoid a collision. The struggle continued under the horse's hoofs and Harry was having some trouble controlling them.

'Be damn careful,' he called down to one of the miners.

'An' if we don't?' the miner shouted back to Harry.

He was near to drawing his pistol, but then he thought the fella must have been cheating at cards like he had been when they first met.

He pulled his horse clear of the trouble and got over to the other side of the street. The miners got a length of rail from somewhere and were trying to force the gambler to straddle it. Thinking he had seen enough, Harry gigged his horse to the edge of town. As he reached the edge of town, he heard a gunshot. He turned to see one of the miners pulling himself away from the struggle. The gambler was holding a smoking gun. The miners were backing off.

Harry dug his spurs into his horse's flanks and went on. Just beyond the edge of town a horse raced by, its rider brandishing a pistol. Harry grinned. The gambler had escaped a tarring and feathering. A minute later, he disappeared up the trail.

Harry pushed on. He went up the trail for a spell. The day had brightened considerably and the sun was filtering through the leafless trees. A pistol shot came from among the trees. Quickly, Harry reached for his gun, and gigged his horse to the side of the trail. Up ahead he could see something lying in the middle of the trail. He squinted, trying to make out what it was. It was the horse the gambler had ridden out on. Harry pulled out his gun.

'Sit still and put that gun away.' The gambler stepped out from behind a tree, holding his pistol.

'Nice to meet you again,' Harry said, putting his gun away.

A big smile cut across the handsome, tanned features of the gambler. 'We met when those miners were trying to tar and feather me, didn't we?'

'Yeah,' Harry said raising his hand. 'I guess we met some place else,' he said to the gambler.

The lean gambler grinned. 'You've got a good memory, my friend. We met when those two youngsters were bright enough to spot me drawing aces out of my sleeve.'

'I remember,' Harry said slowly.

'A right smart pair of boys. You parted company from them?' the gambler asked.

'They're dead,' Harry said quietly.

The gun lowered a mite, as the gambler took in what Harry had said. 'I'm real sorry about that,' he said, and looked as though he meant it. 'They seemed a couple of nice young fellas. What happened? Another falling-out over a deck of cards.'

Shaking his head, Harry said, 'They were in the wrong place at the wrong time.'

'Damn shame. My name's Brett Halliday. You got a name?'

'Harry Rodriguez. I'm a horse trader.'

'Why don't you put your hands down? I ain't gonna shoot you,' Brett told him.

Feeling relieved, Harry lowered his hands. 'What are you going to do?' he asked.

Brett smiled. 'I'm short on cash, but long on horse sense.'

'I know the sort of horse sense you're long on,' Harry told him.

Brett gave a grin. 'You do me an injustice,' he laughed. 'I'll cut you for one of those horses,' he said.

'I might as well give you one of my horses,' Harry said.

'That's cruel, Harry,' the gambler said. 'I've got a gun. I could take one.'

'I guess you could at that.' Harry smiled at the gambler's nerve.

'Now, do you want to step down while I get the cards ready?' Brett asked.

'Sure. Why not?' Harry replied, swinging a leg over the saddle horn, and climbing down.

From the inside of his coat, Brett took a pack of cards and held them out to Harry.

'You cut,' he said.

'That's generous of you.' Lifting about half the pack, Harry showed the seven of diamonds.

'I guess you don't have much luck with cards,' Brett said ruefully.

'Let's see how you do.' Harry put the cards down and watched the gambler's face. He could read nothing.

'Damn shame,' Brett said as he showed the three of spades. 'Care to make it the best of three?'

'No, I don't care to make it the best of three,' Harry said.

'I've still got the gun,' Brett reminded him.

'I thought southern gamblers were men of honour,' Harry said.

Brett roared with laughter. 'Somebody's been telling you some stories. Now, are you going to sell me a horse or do I take one?'

'I'll sell you one.' Harry got up off the tree stump he had been sitting on.

'Mind if I take my pick?' Brett asked him, going over to the horses.

'You can take any, except the brown mare. That's mine. OK?' Harry said, as Brett ran his hand down the flank of the mare.

'You must have owned a couple in your time,' Harry said.

'No, but I've ridden out of town on one or two that weren't my own. You get to know the finer points of a horse that way,' Brett told him. 'Mind if I take the black. I reckon she's got more staying power than the other.'

'And you'd need a horse with staying power the way you play cards,' Harry told him.

'Damn right I would,' Brett laughed again. 'Now, the vexed question of payment. I don't suppose you'd take a bankers' draft?'

'I don't suppose I would, but I might take twenty dollars in paper money or gold,' Harry said, taking out a pencil and piece of paper.

'What's that for?' Brett asked.

'I don't want you hanging for a horse-thief. A card sharp might fit the bill, I reckon.'

'It's a damn shame we're goin' our separate ways. I reckon we could have got on just jim-dandy.' Brett took a billfold out of his pocket, peeled off two tens, and handed them over to Harry.

'Which way did you say you were going?' Brett asked, as he climbed up into the saddle of his new horse.

Harry pointed to the top of the mountains. 'Up and over,' he said.

'Any place in particular?' the gambler asked.

'No, just into the valley so I can start catching some horses in the spring. What about you?' Harry asked.

'Me? I'm just looking for a poker game where the other players have slow minds and slower horses.' Brett pulled a cigar case from his pocket, and handed it to Harry. For a moment, Harry considered it then took a cigar out of it They looked expensive, like everything about Brett Halliday.

Brett bit the end off his and lit it. Then he lit Harry's. They rode in silence for a while.

'Would you care to tell me what happened to them two boys?'

'I guess so,' Harry said, as the memory came back.

'Sounds a damn shame,' Brett replied, blowing out a banner of blue smoke.

'Sure was,' Harry said.

'You any idea who they were?' Brett asked.

'The sheriff down at Beaver reckons it was Slim Loxton and his gang.' Harry flicked the ash off the end of his cigar.

'There's a price on their heads,' Brett said.

'You know them?' Harry asked.

'We crossed paths a while back. Now they're in this neck of the woods.'

'Yeah,' Harry said.

'Then what do you say we go look for them? There's a million poker games going on in this world. I guess they can wait until I'm ready for them.'

Brett tossed his cigar into a pool of water by the side of the trail.

'Hold on, *amigo*. I said that to the sheriff down in Beaver, but I ain't no gunslinger. And there's three of them,' Harry protested.

'Hell, Harry, you don't have to be no gunslinger, just a mite sharper in the head. Most outlaws are fools, otherwise they'd be gamblers.' Brett stroked his horse's neck.

'Like you?' Harry asked him.

'Sure like me,' Brett said with a laugh.

'I'll think it over,' Harry told his companion.

Five minutes later, Brett asked, 'Have you thought it over?'

'I'll try it,' Harry replied.

'Fine. Where did you say you'd seen them?' A smile crossed Brett's lips.

'Not far. Just up here a mite.' Harry pointed to a rise in the ground.

They headed off in that direction, with Harry leading the way. When they got to the top of the rise, Harry reined in, and examined the ground.

'It must have been further up this way,' he said to Brett.

'If you say so,' Brett replied.

'Found it.' Harry pointed to a mess of churned-up hoof marks.

'They're heading up this way,' Brett called out, having ridden on a few yards.

Harry galloped after him.

When they got there, Harry scouted the tracks. 'They were sure in a hurry,' he said.

Both men were riding close together, following the trail up among the rocks. They came to a clearing and Harry called a halt.

'I buried Billy and Frank over there,' he said. Brett did not reply, but just looked in the direction Harry was pointing. They moved on up among the rocks and wild trees.

'Look,' Harry said, indicating the ground below him.

SIX

'OK, little lady, time to git going,' Corey said, pulling at Kate's arm, Kate pulled herself away. Corey was the one she was most frightened of. The one she dreaded being left alone with.

She went outside the cabin. Loxton and Webb were in the saddle.

Loxton, holding on to the leathers of Kate's horse, was impatient to be off. As she put her foot in the stirrup, she felt Corey's hand under her arm.

'Keep your damn hands to yourself,' she snapped at him.

'Leave it, Corey. We've got a fair way to go. Shacktown ain't just over the hill,' Loxton barked. 'Now, let's git.'

Kate pulled herself up into the saddle and clutched at the leathers. The party moved away from the cabin and headed up into the mountains. None of them spoke as they were going.

As far as Kate could judge, they travelled until midday. Then they came to a set of old buildings with smoke rising straight up into the grey sky.

'Are we there?' Kate asked Barney Webb as they swung down out of their saddles.

'No, not by a long way,' Webb said to her. 'We're just stopping off for some provisions. There's not many that knows this place.' He tied his horse to the hitch rail and followed Loxton and Corey inside. The place was dark, and Kate had difficulty seeing anything, until her eyes got used to the gloom. Half a dozen people were sitting round playing cards.

They all turned to watch the newcomers. One or two nodded in Loxton's direction and mumbled greetings. Loxton and the others returned their greetings and went to lounge against the bar.

'Whiskey,' Loxton told the man behind the bar.

The fella moved away to get the drinks. When he came back he looked at Kate.

'What about her?' he asked.

'Better give her a whiskey. It looks like it's gonna be cold agin,' Loxton rasped out.

The barkeep filled out a glass and put it down in front of Kate, who said nothing.

'You'd better drink it,' Loxton told her. 'We've got a ways to go before nightfall, and yer gonna be feelin' cold.'

Picking up the glass, Kate sniffed at it for a moment. It was sickening. Often, Fred would have a drink at the end of a long day. Usually, it was the best brandy. This was the vilest whiskey possible. She smelled it again and gagged on it.

'Don't be so dainty,' Corey chided her. 'Drink it down. Like Slim said, it's gonna be cold up there.'

Once again, Kate put the glass to her mouth and gagged. She could see the others were watching her. This time, she let a mite through her lips. It burned the back of her throat and made her feel sick. The red colour swarmed up her face.

'Finish it off,' Loxton told her, not taking his eyes off her.

'Marty,' Loxton called out suddenly. 'Fix us up some supplies to get us to Shacktown.'

'What are you goin' up there for?' Marty asked, looking at Kate.

'We got some sellin' to do,' Loxton said, throwing a glance Kate's way.

'Should get a fair price for her,' Marty said, leaning against the bar. His face was an inch from Kate's. His breath smelled almost as bad as the whiskey. The stubble on his face was grey and thick. 'Maybe you should stay here overnight,' he said with a grin.

The whiskey had worked its way into Kate's blood. 'Maybe you'd like to take a two-day bath and have a good long shave,' she said.

Loxton and Marty burst out laughing. Behind the bar Marty doubled up, a long racking cough choking off his laughter.

'That'll teach you,' Webb shouted from a table near the back.

Everybody in the room laughed as well.

'When you've straightened yourself out, git them supplies together. We want to make some miles before night.' Loxton poured himself another drink from the bottle on the counter.

'Yeah,' Marty wheezed as he went into the storeroom at the back.

'You'd better finish that whiskey,' Loxton told Kate. 'We're gonna be goin' before too long.'

Kate stared down at the whiskey. Bracing herself, she wrapped her hand round it and took it up to her lips, but lowered it.

'C'mon,' Loxton said. 'We don't want you freezin' to death before we git you there.'

Kate put the glass to her lips again, and took a long swallow. The back of her throat felt like somebody had put a torch to it. She gagged and spluttered then set about coughing. The room exploded with laughter. She put her hands to her stomach.

'Git her outside,' Marty yelled, as he staggered in with a sack full of supplies for the gang.

'Barney, make sure she's all right,' Loxton called between the bouts of laugher. 'We don't want any damaged goods goin' up to Shacktown.'

'OK, boss,' Webb said, as he took hold of Kate and led her out into the cold.

The raw wind hit Kate in the face like a blow from an open hand. She lurched away from Webb as though she was going to fall, but he tightened his grip on her. He pulled her up and led her to the horses.

The smell of the horses and the force of the wind brought Kate to her senses. She stood upright and leaned against the hitch rail, her hand to her mouth.

'You feelin' all right?' Webb asked her.

She shook her head, which was still swimming from the effects of the whiskey. 'I can see what the boss meant by givin' you whiskey like that, it's gonna be damn cold for the next couple of nights.'

'Couple of nights?' Kate told him.

'We should be there in three days,' Webb said. 'Why, have you got some place to go? Because if you have, you'd best forget it. You wouldn't last five minutes out there on yer own.'

Kate had thought a couple of times about making a run for it, but Charlie Salmon's death had made her think again. With Fred lying dead in his grave, she didn't have a lot to go back to. So she was figuring it might be better to die in the mountains than spend her life in Shacktown.

'You feelin' any better?' Webb asked her.

Kate shook her head. 'No, I ain't feelin' any better,' she spluttered.

'Well, you'd better start feelin' better, an' don't take too long about it,' Webb went on.

Behind her Kate heard the door open, and somebody come out.

'Is she any better?' Loxton asked.

'No, but I reckon she can ride, if she has to.'

'She has to,' Loxton said, throwing a sack of supplies over his saddle, and climbing aboard.

Webb helped Kate up, then went round the horses and mounted up himself. Loxton gave the word, and they headed up into the mountains.

Harry and Brett made a thorough search of the cabin they had come across before deciding there was nothing there that would help them. Outside, they found tracks leading up into the mountains.

'This must have been their hideaway. Can't see anybody else using this place,' Brett said.

'Looks like being a long haul. Them tracks are a day old, and it ain't gonna git any easier trackin' them in this weather.' Harry looked up at the snow-filled sky.

'That it ain't,' Brett said drawing the sheepskin coat he had found in the saddle-bag further round him.

Harry grasped the leathers of his horse and pulled himself into the saddle. 'I'm getting too old for this kind of thing,' he told himself.

They gigged their horses and headed up into the mountains.

'You ever been in this part of the country before?' Harry asked his partner.

'No, and I don't intend coming back again.'

It was getting harder and harder to make out tracks as the ground hardened.

'Now what do we do?' Harry asked his companion.

Brett dragged out his last two cigars and handed one to Harry. They lit them up and sat on their horses as they smoked.

'I've got an idea,' Brett said eventually.

'What would that be?' Harry asked, blowing out the blue smoke.

Brett pulled a pack of cards from his pocket and held them out to Harry. 'You cut first.'

Harry cut the pack. Ten of spades.

'Not bad,' Brett said, making his cut.

He came up with a jack of diamonds. They turned north.

Kate Battersby was feeling slightly better. The feeling of sickness in her stomach had subsided and she felt the warmth of the whiskey. The freezing wind had blown itself out a mite. Corey rode beside her. Loxton was in front, with Webb bringing up the rear.

'We should make it in no time at all, now,' Corey said with a hint of relish in his voice.

Kate bit back a sharp answer. Corey was a man who would slap her in the mouth. She still felt scared, but she wasn't going to show it to Corey or any of the others. She tightened her grip on the leathers and tried to think of a way out of the mess she was in.

'What are you thinkin' about?' Corey's voice suddenly broke into her thoughts.

'Nothing,' Kate told him.

'I bet you was tryin' to figure a way out of here?'

Kate bit her lip and became aware of Corey stiffening in the saddle. Three riders were slowly coming down the trail.

'Well, would you believe it?' Loxton sang out, pointing to the riders.

The lead rider held up his hand in salute. 'Slim Loxton, I'll be damned. This is a fine time and place to meet you.'

'Blade Harris, you old son-of-a-bitch,' Loxton greeted the man.

Harris sat astride a grey gelding, his hat pulled over his ears and held down by a scarf. He laughed heartily, rode up to Loxton and greeted him with a warm handshake. Webb had caught up with Kate and Corey. He had a suspicious look on his face.

'What do you reckon that sidewinder wants?' he asked Corey.

'I don't know, but I reckon it ain't good. See them critters he's got with him? Mike Day and Jess Garfield. They're bigger rats than he is.' Webb spat in the snow.

Kate watched as Day and Garfield, a mean-looking pair, continued past Loxton and settled beside Corey.

'Where are you takin' this looker?' Day asked, leaning on his saddle horn.

'We're gonna take her up to Shacktown. Slim reckons we'll get a fair price for her,' Corey told him. Kate noticed his hand slipping closer to his gun.

'There's no need fer that,' Garfield said, watching the movement through his half-closed eyes. 'Maybe we could borrow her for a spell. We're all pals. We'd see you got her back in one piece.'

Mike Day laughed as though it was the funniest thing he had heard. 'Yeah, we'd even throw in a few dollars.'

'That we would,' Garfield said.

Kate felt sick as she listened to the conversation. Her hand fastened and unfastened round the leathers. She would have given anything to have had a shotgun. Corey and Webb exchanged glances.

Suddenly, Loxton gigged his horse and pulled ahead. 'You comin'?' he bawled over his shoulder.

'Gotta be goin' boys,' Webb said, and started off after Loxton. 'Be seein' you,' Blade Harris called back.

'What do you reckon he means by that?' Corey asked Webb, as soon as they were out of earshot.

'To my way of thinkin' it's obvious. Slim's turned down the same deal as we got offered. You're in some demand,' he said to Kate.

'Go to hell,' Kate shouted at him, unable to keep her temper in check.

Webb caught Corey's hand as he lashed out. 'Slim wouldn't like you damaging the merchandise,' he said.

'Guess not,' Corey told him.

They rode on through the howling wind. Kate noticed Corey watching the back trail. Eventually, the light began to fail, and Loxton came back towards them.

'There's an old hideout up here a ways,' he said. 'I guess that's where Blade must have come from. He must've been shelterin' from a posse or the weather.'

'Most likely a posse, knowin' Blade,' Corey said.

'Barney, git yourself up there, and git that fire goin'. We don't want Mrs Battersby catching cold, do we?'

'We sure don't,' Webb said with a laugh.

He galloped off down the trail, and cut through the trees.

Ten minutes later, he swung down into a gully where the hideout lay screened by pine trees. Webb lifted the latch and opened the door.

The place smelled of Blade Harris and his boys. The embers of the fire were just dying in the grate. Webb hunkered down and blew on them. They faded, then glowed again.

A flame started to eat into the wood. Quickly, he picked up a few small pieces of wood and tossed them into the fire. The flames licked at them greedily. Soon he had a fair blaze going.

Webb went outside to his horse. Unhitching it, he led it round to the lean-to and unsaddled it. Then he went inside again, with some supplies from the saddle-bag. He pushed back the sacking that was keeping the wind out and saw Loxton and the others.

'What kept you?' he asked jocularly.

'You got that fire going yet?' Loxton asked gruffly, and strode towards the cabin.

'Sure I got it goin'. What do you think I've been doing?' Webb asked angrily.

'Just askin',' Loxton said, going into the cabin. He saw the fire and hunkered down in front of it.

'Did you bring that bottle of whiskey in?' he asked Webb.

'Yeah,' Webb answered him, pulling the cork out and pouring some into a couple of mugs for Corey and Loxton.

'You want some?' he asked Kate.

'You can put some in a mug, but I don't want a lot like last time,' she said.

'Anythin' you say,' Webb laughed.

Kate took the mug from him when he had poured the whiskey.

'When you've warmed yourself up,' Loxton told her. 'Git some chow goin'. Webb'll show you where the stuff is,' he growled.

Kate took her time in drinking the whiskey. She followed Webb into the back where he laid out some grub ready for cooking. After they had eaten, the three men took out a deck of cards and started playing. It was a noisy game, and Kate put it down to the whiskey they had drunk. She watched and listened, hoping they would fall asleep before they had any thoughts about her. Eventually, they started to yawn, and Loxton produced a rope from somewhere.

'I don't think you'd be tempted to run out on us tonight, but just in case you are, I'm gonna tie you to the bed.'

The rope bit into her wrists as he lashed them together. Corey and Webb were snoring on the other side of the room.

The snoring of the three men lasted until the sun came up. Kate had slept fitfully. Just after dawn she heard a noise outside. Then she heard the jingling of spurs.

Loxton stopped snoring and shifted in his bed. Like a restless animal, he slowly raised his head. A second later a shot slapped into the doorframe. Webb and Corey were awake in seconds, their guns in their hands.

'Glad yer awake,' Blade Harris called out as another slug smashed into the wood. 'I hate killin' sleepin' men, especially when they're friends of mine.'

'Go to hell, Blade, An' yer no friend of mine,' Loxton called out as another bullet slammed into the door.

'Hold it,' Day yelled. 'There ain't no sense

wastin' lead. Just send the little lady out, and we'll just go away, honest. Guess you boys have had yer fun with her by now.'

'If you want her,' Corey yelled, 'come an' get her.'

'If you don't send her out, she'll be yer meal-ticket to hell!' Blade Harris shouted back, and sent a couple of slugs through the wood of the door.

SEVEN

'Damn noisy hereabouts,' Harry said, pushing his hat clear of his eyes as the exchange of shots continued. He stood up and rubbed his back, trying to ease the ache brought on by the cold.

Brett got up as well and shivered. 'There's no consideration around here for a body who needs his beauty sleep. Who do you reckon it is?'

Harry scratched his head. 'I wouldn't be a million miles out if I said it was them fellas we'd been chasin'. Maybe they've run into a posse,' he said, opening the chamber of his .45 and checking the loads. Brett did the same, then took out a small-calibre pistol from the inside of his coat pocket and checked it.

'Let's make a start,' Harry said, gathering up the leathers. They decided to walk in the direction of the gunfire, hoping to surprise whoever it was that was doing the shooting. They moved through the undergrowth, their hands over their horses' mouths, until they could see the cabin that Blade Harris and his boys were firing into.

'Blade's really got them pinned down,' Brett said.

'You know him?' Harry asked.

'He's a fella I played a hand of poker against last Fall, and has probably got Mike Day and Jess Garfield with him. I can still see his gun under my nose. Luckily, divine providence in the form of a soiled dove, got me out of it. Lord bless her,' Brett said with a smile.

'Let's get down there. They've still got that woman, and maybe she's gettin' shot up as well.'

'If Blade's prowess with a gun is equal to his prowess with a deck of cards, I'd reckon she's pretty safe,' Brett replied.

'If his prowess with a gun has improved, she's not gonna be safe,' Harry said.

'If you put it that way, we'd better get down there, but take it easy. I've seen three of them,' Brett said.

They hitched their horses to a tree, and started off down the gully. The slope was wet and slippery, and both men had a hard time keeping their feet.

At the bottom, Brett pointed to Day, who was crouched behind a tree stump, pressing fresh loads into his gun. He was unaware of the two men, until Brett's gun descended on the back of his head. Harry stuffed Day's bandanna into his mouth, and tied his hands behind his back with his own bandanna.

'Over there,' Brett said, pointing to where Garfield was kneeling behind a rock.

Fire was being returned at a pretty steady rate from the cabin.

'It doesn't look as though Blade Harris is getting all his own way,' Harry murmured.

'No, it doesn't,' Brett agreed. 'Got any bright ideas?'

The fire continued for a spell, then slackened.

'Something's going on down there,' Brett said to his partner.

There was a silence as a figure ran across the clearing holding a firebrand.

'Things are hotting up down there,' Brett said, spinning the chamber of his .45.

'Looks as though we're going to have to do something about it,' Harry said as Jess Garfield tossed the brand at the porch and dodged his way back to some cover, followed by a hail of bullets.

Brett aimed at Garfield, who had got himself behind a tree. He sent a bullet his way. The wood splintered, and Garfield turned, a look of surprise on his face. Garfield and Harris looked up towards the cover that Harry and Brett were using. At the same time, Loxton and the others must have realized that that somebody up there was giving them some help.

The door of the cabin opened quickly, and Webb dashed on to the veranda to grab the blazing torch. He threw it clear of the cabin so that it sizzled out in the snow. As he turned to run back inside, a bullet clipped his leg and sent him tumbling back over the threshold. The door was slammed shut straight away.

Garfield suddenly broke clear and ran to where Day was tied up, and cut him loose. The two ducked and weaved their way back to some cover.

From where he was, Harry could see that Blade Harris and his boys were in a fix. The firing from the cabin had increased. Blade Harris called out something and raised his arms. The three men suddenly broke cover and ran for their horses. Silence hung over the place after the three men had galloped out.

'Now, all we've got to do is get Mrs Batttersby out,' Brett said.

Harry watched as a door was opened and a head was stuck out.

A second later a white flag appeared, and Slim Loxton walked out, his hands held up.

'What do you want?' Harry shouted down to him.

'We ain't got a beef with you,' Loxton replied.

'Mrs Battersby's husband's sure got a beef with you. So you can start by sending her out. Then you can come out with your hands up.'

'Is that some kind of joke?' Loxton put his hand to his mouth to make sure the sound carried up the hill.

'No, it ain't no kind of a joke,' Brett called down

to the outlaw. 'You ain't goin' anywhere, except jail.'

'We're holding the ace. So if you want to risk coming down for her, she's all yours. When you get down here, you might find she's got a bullet in her.' He laughed wildly before slipping back into the cabin.

'Got any bright ideas?' Brett asked again, as the door slammed shut.

For a moment Harry thought about it, then said, 'I guess not.'

Brett passed over the case containing the cigars. 'These are the last,' he said after Harry had taken one.

'Damn fine smokes,' Harry said, lighting it and blowing the smoke up in the direction of the grey sky. 'Could be we're heading for more snow.'

'Could be,' Brett agreed with him, following his gaze just as another bullet sliced the crisp air above their heads. Both men rolled clear and got behind some better cover. A couple more shots followed.

'Still plannin' to come down for Mrs Battersby?' Jack Corey shouted up to them.

'We'll be down when we're ready, boys. You just wait there,' Brett called out levering a bullet into the breech of his rifle. He stuck his head over the fallen tree they were sheltering behind. Moments later another shot whipped over his head.

'Close,' he shouted.

'They'll be gettin' closer,' Loxton shouted as he sent up another.

Night was beginning to come on as the clouds were getting thicker and thicker. A freezing wind scudded over the faces of Harry and Brett.

Harry shivered. 'We ain't gonna be able to stay here much longer,' he said.

Brett was thinking much the same thing.

'We'll move back a mite, build ourselves a fire, and fix up some coffee. We'll make it where we can still see them,' Brett said, blowing on his hands.

'Let's git started.' Harry got up slowly so as not to attract another bullet from the cabin. They moved along the narrow trail, keeping the undergrowth between themselves and those below.

'This'll do fine,' Brett said as they reached the end of the trail. He looked round him and started to pick up some wood. 'I'll get a fire goin',' he said. 'You go and get some food and some coffee.'

Harry went back to get the provisions. The horses nickered as he approached them. He felt around in the saddle-bags and took out some coffee and some of the food. Putting the food into the pockets of his sheepskin jacket, he went round to the other side of the horse and took a couple of mugs out of the saddle-bags. As he walked back to the fire, the first flakes of snow began to fall.

Brett was hunkered down, piling more logs on to the growing blaze. He stopped when he heard Harry approach.

'Didn't happen to find any whiskey in the saddle-bags, did you?' he asked, taking the mugs off Harry.

Harry searched his pockets and pulled out a half-bottle of whiskey.

'That's the best I could do,' he said with a grin.

Brett took the bottle and pulled the cork. Then he poured them both a generous measure. Then he started to fix the grub.

'I'm going to take a look and see how things are down there,' Harry told him as he finished the whiskey.

'You won't see much,' Brett said over his shoulder.

Harry walked away. From the top of the hill he thought he could hear raucous laughter from the cabin below. Then he thought it might be the wind. He wondered how Kate Battersby was making out. He blinked against the snow.

'Fixed you up some grub,' a familiar voice behind him said.

Brett stood beside him with a hunk of bacon wrapped in some bread.

'Eat it while it's hot. Anything going on down there?' Brett asked, gesturing towards the cabin.

'No,' Harry said, passing his rifle to Brett, then taking a bite out of the bread and bacon.

'I'll come round with some hot coffee in an hour, then you can turn in and I'll take a watch,' Brett said when Harry had finished eating.

'That'll be fine,' Harry replied, wiping his greasy hands on his jacket.

He turned to see Brett walking down the trail to the fire. Within a second he had disappeared into the fast-swirling flakes of snow.

Harry stamped his feet and slapped his arms against his chest. Then he walked up and down. The snow was falling thicker and faster. The time seemed to be dragging. A couple of times he turned, expecting to see Brett coming towards him, but it was nothing. He wished that Brett had put some more whiskey in the coffee he had brought.

Below him the snow was building up against the side of the cabin. He wondered how long it would be before those inside were snowed in.

If he fell asleep in this storm, he would freeze to death. After a while, Brett came crunching through the snow.

'There's some fresh coffee in the pot, and I've built a lean-to beside one of the trees. You should be able to get some sleep there.'

Harry trudged off through the thickening snow, until he came to the lean-to. Brett had fashioned a break in the roof so that the smoke could get out. Stretching his hands in front of the flames, he let the heat get to them for a few minutes.

The coffee-pot stood beside the fire and next to it stood the half-bottle of whiskey. Harry filled up a mug of coffee, then added some whiskey. With his knife, he cut a piece of bacon off the hunk by the fire. The drink and the coffee made him feel better.

Harry yawned, then lay down using the saddle as a pillow.

He knew something was wrong when he opened his eyes. The horse trader got up and looked round, not that he could see too much in the lean-to. Feeling round, he put his hand on the stock of his Winchester. The light of the moon was filtering through the breaks in the lean-to. Twisting on to his belly, he crawled outside. The first thing he got was a mouthful of snow, falling from the branch of a tree. Clearing out his mouth and hair, he put on his hat and cautiously got to his feet.

He listened to the wind for a spell as it blew through the trees, then he heard the branches creaking under the weight of the snow. Harry started to run along the trail. His foot caught in a branch and he fell headlong into the snow.

The Winchester flew out of his hands. Harry pulled himself to his feet. He swore. It wasn't a tree root that he had fallen over; it was the half-covered body of Brett.

Pushing the snow off the back of Brett's head, Harry reached along his neck until he found a pulse. He felt the cold, sticky blood that had started to congeal among Brett's thick, brown hair.

'Come on,' he said as the wind started to rise again. Hooking his fingers under Brett's collar, he pulled the unconscious gambler to his feet. Slinging him over his shoulder, he picked up the Winchester and started back down the trail to the lean-to.

Harry gasped as he struggled through the snow with Brett. When he got him to the lean-to, he laid Brett down and pulled him inside. The first thing Harry did was put more logs on the fire until it started to burn up again. By its light, he examined Brett's face. The flesh was pale with the cold. Picking up the whiskey, Harry raised Brett's head and put it under his nose. For a moment, nothing happened, and then the gambler's nose twitched and the colour returned to the edges of his face.

'Take it easy, partner,' Harry whispered, tipping the bottle to Brett's lips.

The gambler's eyes flickered slowly, and then opened. He looked round.

'Pity you didn't get up here a mite sooner. We'd have had them cold.' He grinned painfully.

'Sorry about that, but I was catching up on some beauty sleep.'

Again, Harry passed the whiskey to Brett's lips. The gambler took a swallow, then coughed.

'You look as though you can use all the beauty sleep you can get,' he chuckled.

'When you're ready you can tell me what happened, but you don't have to be a smart southern gambler to work it out,' Harry said.

'No, I guess you don't,' Brett gasped. 'Did I finish all that whiskey?'

'No, there are a couple of mouthfuls left,' Harry smiled, and tilted the bottle to Brett's lips again. 'You badly hurt?'

'Hell, no. I just took the stock of a rifle on the back of my head,' Brett said, licking his lips.

'We ain't gonna be able to follow them now.'

For a moment both men were silent.

'Guess it's gonna have to be a good night's sleep,' Harry said.

Slim Loxton was hunched low in the saddle, his face muffled against the driving snow and biting wind. Behind him rode Kate Battersby, her hands tied to the pommel of the saddle and a gag round her mouth. Barney Webb followed her, then came Jack Corey, occasionally checking the back trail.

Loxton had seen how things were going outside the cabin. The snow was being driven hard against the walls and it would not be long before they had to dig themselves out.

'This is the way it's gonna be, boys,' he had said. 'We're gonna tie her to the saddle, gag her and ride out of here. It's gonna be tough in this snow, but it's gonna be our best chance of getting out without too much fuss.'

Nobody liked the idea much, but then nobody could think of a better one.

Loxton moved over to Kate's side. 'Like I said,

you're gonna be gagged, so don't even try to breathe loud.'

Kate looked terrified.

'You're worth more to us alive than dead, but our real need is to get out of this rat-trap in one piece. Understand what I'm tellin' you?'

Kate nodded her head, her eyes wide with fear.

They had gone outside at just the same time that Harry and Brett had been swapping places.

'As near as I can figure it, they're up there between that pine and that rock. Can you see it?'

Webb and Corey had nodded.

'I'll take the lead,' Loxton had said, swinging up into the saddle. Then they headed up the trail.

He had hoped to swing wide of the rock, but the trail narrowed and was flanked by snow-covered scrub. He had signalled to Corey to come up.

'I think I got him. Get up there and quieten him. Don't care how you do it, just make it quiet and quick.'

Corey dismounted and hauled his Winchester out of its saddle holster. His eyes squinted against the snow as he edged down the trail.

A few yards in front of him, he saw the figure of Brett Halliday, looking down towards the cabin. Brett remained where he was for a moment, then started to walk up and down, stamping his feet on the ground.

Corey edged closer, almost stopping breathing as he did so. Brett stopped and stood facing away from Corey. Corey moved quickly, bringing his rifle up, and swinging it down. He felt satisfied when Brett grunted and hit the ground. Corey went back the way he had come.

'Fixed him,' he had said.

'Good,' Loxton had replied.

'Let's git goin' before this snow stops,' Loxton called without turning round. He dug his spurs into his horse's flanks and moved out.

'We're in a hole now.' Brett sat against his saddle, a bandage tied round his head. His cold fingers were wrapped around the mug of coffee that Harry had made for him.

'Got any ideas?' he asked, putting it to his lips.

'We know they're heading up country, so wherever they're going it must be up there somewhere,' Harry said, putting his mug to his lips, 'This ain't a part of the country I've been in before. Well, not all that often.'

Brett shook his head. 'Like I said, I've never visited here.'

The men looked at each other.

'Guess the only thing to do is to just keep on going. How are we fixed for grub?' Harry asked his companion.

'We won't be having any big parties,' Brett told him. 'So long as we're careful, we should be OK.'

Outside, it was completely white and there was an eerie silence about the landscape. Harry felt

like a ghost as he climbed into the saddle.
Hauling on the leathers, he guided his horse up
towards the crest of the mountain.

EIGHT

Barney Webb was scratching at his leg. The bandage he had put on it didn't seem to be doing it any good. Slim Loxton was up ahead, leading Kate Battersby's horse. Jack Corey was behind him, scouting the back trail.

'We gonna stop for some grub?' he hollered up to Loxton.

Loxton turned in his saddle. 'Give it another hour or so, then we'll bed down for the night.' His big hand wiped the snow off his shoulder. They had pushed on through the blizzard, hoping to lose the men who had been firing at them.

'We don't want to be turnin' round an' findin' them on our heels,' he shouted back to Corey.

'You got any idea who them buzzards was?' Corey shouted up to him.

'No, I ain't, but if I run across them, they won't be shootin' at anybody else for a spell,' Loxton bawled back.

Kate Batttersby shivered. Loxton had taken the gag out of her mouth and loosened the ropes round her wrists. The cold had cut through her clothes and was making her bones ache. She was getting tired. It was the kind of tiredness that sucked the life out of a body. She hunched over in the saddle, and shucked the blanket further round her shoulders. Kate fought hard to keep her eyes open. Gradually, the lids became heavier and heavier until they closed. The horse she was riding lurched on the snow-covered ground, throwing her to one side.

Instinctively, she tightened her grip on the leathers. Kate's eyes opened quickly, The ground reeled. She gritted her teeth. She wasn't going to give them the satisfaction of hearing her call for a halt.

Loxton looked back at her. 'You all right?' He sounded like a banker protecting his investment.

'Yes, I'm all right,' she replied, looking across at him.

'Suit yourself,' he told her with an ugly tone in his voice.

Kate watched him with a growing fire burning inside her. During the morning they went on through the deep snow. Then it started to come down again. Loxton called a halt.

Harry and Brett called a halt at roughly the same time, built some shelter and lit a fire, then settled down to a scanty meal and turned in for a couple of hours.

'How long will it be before we get there?' Kate asked apprehensively. Her worried eyes scanned the top of the mountain.

Anytime now, they would reach the crest of the mountain and begin the descent to Shacktown. A couple of times, she had heard the men talking about how much they would get for her. She shuddered at the thought of her fate.

Slim Loxton turned to her, an evil grin on his face. 'Mighty anxious to see what yer new owner's gonna look like,' he chided her. 'Well, we'll be startin' down the other side, an' it's half a day from there.'

Kate took a pull from the coffee he had handed her. Its warmth was the only thing that cheered her. She gave Loxton a sideways glance, then looked across to the horses. She thought about making a break for it.

'I don't think you'd make it,' Loxton said to her. 'I'd just catch you and then make sure you didn't run away from anybody else. I'd cut one of yer hamstrings.' He laughed and turned to where the others were breaking down the shelter they had fixed up.

While Webb was kicking out the marks they had made in the snow, Kate noticed that he was still limping and blood was seeping through his trousers. Corey had put a heap of snow over the fire and was saddling the horses.

'You boys about ready?' Loxton shouted across to them.

'Yeah, boss,' Webb said, rubbing his leg. He got himself up into the saddle. Corey did the same.

'Come on,' Loxton said, taking the mug from Kate and grabbing her elbow. He pulled her over to the horses, then stood behind her while she mounted up.

He kicked the flanks of his horse and rode up the steepening trail. The others followed them out. The horses moved laboriously up the slope. The wind rose and howled at them. Kate sat in the saddle and shivered. Behind her, Barney Webb was starting to feel some real pain in his leg. Jack Corey rode on, indifferent to the cold and thinking of the whiskey and the women they could buy with the money they got from selling Kate Battersby.

They hit the top of the rise and started down, riding between the trees that flanked the trail, their branches weighed down with the snow. The trees hemmed them in. Once or twice a heap of snow fell off the branches, narrowly missing the riders. Kate had expected some shelter from the wind on the downward journey, but it didn't happen. With each step the horse took, the wind seemed to come at them with even more savagery. It bit at the flanks of the horse and once or twice Kate felt as though her own horse would go toppling over and throw her into the snow. It was the worst part of the journey so far.

Loxton hauled on the leathers of his horse, guiding it downwards to the valley floor. The slope flattened a mite and the horse became more sure of its footing. The snowfall lessened and there came the occasional break in it, so that Kate could see the valley floor. Then she saw the buildings, snow-covered humps on the ground.

'We're there,' Loxton called over his shoulder, with a cheerful grin on his face. They moved along the trail. As they rounded a bend, she saw the first buildings. Thick, black smoke was pouring from their chimneys and was being whipped round by the wind. Loxton led her horse down a narrow alley, then dismounted and lifted the latch on the gate. A heap of snow fell off the gate. It groaned as Loxton pushed it open. Webb and Corey followed them in.

'Git down,' Loxton told her.

Stiffly, Kate swung herself down. Behind her she heard a door open. Two men came out into the yard. They were muffled-up pretty tight. The first man held a lantern raised high in his left hand. He held a pistol in his right. His companion held a shotgun. The men moved closer.

'That any way to greet an' old pal?' Loxton called out to them.

The man with the pistol lowered it a mite and laughed.

'Hi, Slim,' he yelled. He pulled down the scarf so that it uncovered his face. Holding out his hand to Loxton, he stepped forward.

'Hi, Sam,' Loxton said, affably, holding out his own hand. Sam grabbed it and shook it warmly.

'Hi, boys,' he greeted the other two. 'Who's the lady?' he asked, walking over to Kate.

'I'll tell you inside. We didn't come up here to freeze to death!' Loxton laughed and slapped Sam's shoulder.

'Danny, take care of them horses,' Sam called out to the other fella.

'Anythin' you say, boss,' Danny said, lowering the shotgun and leading Loxton's horse over to the barn.

Sam led them inside, with Kate following Loxton. They went down a dark corridor, lit only by a few lamps hanging on the walls. The walls creaked as the wind beat against them. The place smelled bad. Kate almost collided with Loxton as they came into the main room. From what she could see, the place was some kind of a saloon. As her eyes grew used to the gloom, she could make out men and women sitting at the tables playing cards.

Sam moved round to the business end of the bar, and put a bottle and four glasses on the counter.

'Want some grub?' he asked.

'Sure could do with some. We need something to

keep out the cold, along with the whiskey,' Loxton said, filling out the four glasses. The other two had followed them in, and were ranged along the bar.

Pulling off his coat, Loxton dropped it, along with Corey's and Webb's, on a nearby chair.

'You'd better do the same,' he said to Kate. 'You want some of this?' he asked, holding the bottle up.

'A drop,' Kate told him, thinking of the last time she had had whiskey.

'Too strong for you?' a voice behind her asked, making her start.

'Leave her alone, Marlene,' Loxton said threateningly.

Turning, Kate watched as the blonde-haired Marlene moved towards her, ignoring Loxton's warning.

'Hi, Marlene,' Webb and Corey sang out.

'Nice to see you boys again,' Marlene said to them. 'You brought her up here to sell?' She turned to face Loxton.

'We sure have. Reckon me an' the boys could make a few hundred, maybe a thousand,' Loxton said, as he took a drink of whiskey.

Marlene's hand reached out quickly for Kate's arm. She squeezed it. 'Not much muscle,' she said, when she had let go of it. 'Nice and soft, though. Yeah, you boys'll make yer money on her.'

Kate backed away, her face white. Marlene

glared at her then threw the remains of her drink in her face. She reached out to strike her, but Loxton caught hold of her wrist and twisted it brutally. Marlene let out a scream as she tried to pull away from Loxton, but he was ready for her. He twisted her arm again so that she was forced down on her knees.

She swore viciously as Loxton pushed her away. She sprawled across the floor in an untidy heap. Loxton's boys laughed. The others in the saloon laughed along with them.

'You bastard!' Marlene screamed as she struggled to her feet.

Kate felt sorry for her. She bent down and put her hand under Marlene's to help her up.

Marlene glared at her venomously, and roughly pulled herself away. 'Keep yer damned hands off me,' she screamed.

Quickly, like a cat, she got to her feet, and ran for the door at the far end of the bar. A moment later, the door slammed shut behind her.

From the other side of the door Marlene could hear them laughing at her. Rubbing her wrists, she ran up the stairs to her room. It was dark. Scrabbling around, she found the matches, and lit the lamp. The pale, yellow light gave little illumination to the room. Marlene flung herself down on the bed, tears of rage and humiliation welling up in her blue eyes. Once upon a time, she had loved Slim Loxton. Now, she hated him, and the girl he had brought up to the town to sell. She had known that Slim Loxton had never really loved her. As long as she could see him occasionally, and he treated her right, she had not minded.

She would kill the girl. Her rage knew no bounds. It was as though something had snapped in her mind. She lay on the bed fuming and fretting.

Downstairs, Loxton and his pals had stopped laughing, and were digging into the food. Kate sat at the back of the room watching them and worrying. She was worrying about what was going to happen to her after she had been sold at the auction. She could see no way of getting clear of the place, getting away from Loxton and his cronies, not unless the weather cleared up, and the snow melted away. She could feel them watching her all the time they ate their food and drank their whiskey.

The small amount of whiskey she had drunk had warmed her, and then she forced herself to eat something. A couple of times Corey had offered her another drink, but she had refused. Loxton had given him a hard look when he had done that.

When he had finished eating, he looked round at her.

'Had enough to eat?' he asked.

'Yes,' answered Kate.

'Sam,' Loxton called over the bar, as Corey and

Webb poured themselves more drink.

'Yeah?' Sam came across wiping his hands on the cloth. 'What can I do for you?'

'You got some place where we can leave Mrs Battersby fer the night?' Preferably some place Marlene can't get at her to scratch her eyes out.'

Sam laughed and flung the cloth on the bar. 'Sure, I got somewhere like that.'

'An' it had better be warm, we don't want Mrs Battersby comin' down with pneumonia. Do we, honey?'

Kate ignored the remark.

'Yeah, it's nice an' warm. Come on, baby,' Sam said to her.

Reluctantly, Kate got out of her chair and followed him. He led her out of the bar and through a door at the opposite side of the passage to the door that Marlene had run through. The short corridor was dark. A flight of stairs ran upwards. Taking a lamp from the wall, he led her up the stairs to a room at the end of the corridor. Unlocking the door, he handed her the lamp.

'I reckon this is what Slim had in mind,' he said.

With that he closed the door, and Kate heard the key turn in the lock. She looked round. The room was a small one, with a window in the back wall. Kate hunkered down in front of the fire and warmed her hands. She rubbed them together to get the circulation going again. After ten minutes, she got up. There was a table, a chair and a single bed. She walked over to the window. Wiping the dust off with her scarf, she could see that it was still snowing pretty hard.

For the first time since she had been kidnapped, she thought of the ranch. She pressed her hands to her face and started to cry, something that she had promised herself that she would not do, no matter what. In the end she came away from the window and lay down on the bed. It took her a long time to get to sleep.

NINE

'There's a light coming from down there,' Harry said, hauling on the leathers of his horse. Brett came up alongside him and looked down into the valley.

'You're damn right, partner,' he said. 'We'd better get down there and see if there's any shelter for us. Another night of this will be the end of me.'

Both men nudged their horse's flanks and headed down the trail.

They hit the valley floor a mile from where Loxton and his buddies had come down on to it. They hitched their horses to a rail outside a saloon and pushed their way in through the batwing doors. The place was empty.

'Ghost saloon,' Brett said, as he pulled off his gloves, and smacked them down on the bar. As he spoke a door at the far end of the saloon opened, and an elderly barkeep came out from the back.

'What'll it be, gents?' he asked. His voice sounded suspicious and he was watching them closely.

'A couple of whiskeys,' Brett said. 'And some grub, if you've got it.'

'Yeah, I can do you some grub,' the barkeep told him, as he filled up a couple of glasses and set them down.

Brett looked round the saloon after he had put his drink down in one.

'Not much trade in tonight,' he observed.

'No, there ain't,' the barkeep replied.

'Any particular reason for that?' Harry asked.

The barkeep eyed them both and thought about it.

'Well, it can't do any harm,' he said. 'Most of my clientele have moved out since the new town down the trail opened up,' He wiped a few glasses, while he thought some more.

'Yer kinda strugglin' fer words,' Harry said to him.

'Yeah, that I am,' the barkeep said, putting down the cloth. 'There's some real bad *hombres* bin moving into that town. An' no sheriff to keep any kinda order.'

'What kinda real bad *hombres*?' Brett held out his glass for a refill.

The barkeep turned. He took a bottle from the shelf, and filled up Brett's glass, and then Harry's. When he had finished, he put the cork back in the bottle. 'Outlaws, any kinda real bad *hombres*,' he said.

'Is it the kinda, place you'd bring a woman if you had taken her from her husband?' Brett asked the man.

The man eyed him sharply. 'Yeah, it's that kinda place. They'd probably get some money for her.'

'Get some money for her?' Harry asked in surprise.

'Sure. They sell any woman that ain't got no owner. Any fella could buy her if he's of a mind to. That's when she becomes his property,' the barkeep said, watching their faces. 'Looks like you gents ain't ever heard of this place.'

Brett and Harry exchanged glances.

'No, we ain't ever heard of this kinda place,' Harry said.

'We've led a very sheltered upbringing,' Brett told the barkeep.

'You sure look like you've led a sheltered upbringing,' he told them.

'This town that's just down the trail, how far down the trail is it?' Harry said, taking a drink from the glass.

'A couple of miles down. Maybe three,'

'You got some place fer us to bed down for the night?" Harry asked the barkeep.

'I sure have, but it's gonna cost you though. There's some food out back, and some breakfast in the morning. Just as soon as the weather clears up, I'll be heading out myself. There ain't anybody left to serve.'

'As long as you git to servin' us first,' Harry said. 'Say, what's yer name?'

'Hal Roberts,' the barkeep said.

Both men sat down near the fire and waited for Hal to serve their food. Harry yawned, leaned forward in his chair and pulled off his sheepskin jacket.

A minute later, Brett did the same,

'Heat gettin' to you boys'?' Hal asked, coming in with the food.

'Yeah, it's the warmest I've bin since. . . .' Harry's voice trailed off. He had been about to say, 'The warmest I've bin since I burned my cabin.'

'You got any particular reason for going to Shacktown – that's the name of the place? Only you don't look like the kind of gents who'd be welcome there.'

Brett and Harry exchanged glances.

'I don't figure you're on the run from the law. You don't look like bounty hunters either.' Hal pulled up a chair and sat down.

'We're lookin' for somebody,' Brett said, between mouthfuls. 'A woman by the name of Kate Battersby. Slim Loxton and his gang kidnapped her off the Beaver stage.'

'Slim Loxton,' Hal echoed. 'That's the kinda place you'd find him. Come to think of it, there's a fella down there that might help you. He's an old buddy of mine. Mort Jackson, He used to work in this place with me. He told me before he left he's got a job down there in some saloon. It's the only work he knows.'

'We'll be lookin' him up,' Brett said.

Kate Battersby was still cold when she woke up, despite the fact she had put more logs on the fire to keep it going. She blew on the embers to get the flames going again.

The footsteps on the stairs startled her. Quickly, she went back to the bed. A key rattled in the lock.

'Some hot grub for you,' Sam told her, laying the tray down on the rough table.

'I'm obliged,' Kate said in a sulky tone.

Sam looked at her and laughed, 'Somebody will whip that tone out of you pretty soon,' he said. 'If somebody from round here doesn't buy you, then maybe the boss will. We need some new gals in this place.'

Kate looked at the tray.

'Don't worry, it won't be for a day or two yet. Give you time to get some rest and pretty yerself up. Enjoy your food,' he said as he went out.

When he had gone, Kate sat for a while on the bed. Pulling the cloth from the plate, she remembered how hungry she was. She examined what was on the plate. It looked like some kind of vegetables and some kind of meat. She picked up the eating irons and poked at it. It was sloppy and messy, but it didn't smell too bad. Cautiously, she put her fork into it, moved it round on her plate, then put some into her mouth. At least, she thought, it didn't taste too bad. Her appetite whetted, she ate quickly and hungrily. By the time she had eaten all the food she was feeling better.

She paced up and down the room, in an effort to get warmer and to try to figure a way of helping herself. She went to the window. The day had brightened up considerably and it was getting warmer outside. She noticed that the snow had started to melt. Maybe she would think of something.

Slim Loxton was lounging in the saloon bar, just having eaten breakfast. He was waiting for Corey to come downstairs. Webb had gone to see the doctor to get his leg fixed up, it having taken bad ways. Corey came down and greeted him.

'Fix yerself up some breakfast,' Loxton told him. 'Sam's gone to feed Mrs Battersby.'

'How long do you reckon we're gonna be here, boss?' Corey shouted from the kitchen as he put his bacon and beans on a plate. 'Place ain't got much life to it.'

'Sure hasn't,' Loxton called back. 'We ain't gonna be here long. We're just waitin' for the auctioneer.'

'How come I never met this auctioneer fella?' Corey asked, coming through from the kitchen.

'He was still doin' time,' Loxton said finishing his coffee.

'So what's he gonna do now he's back here?' Corey, asked him, following Loxton over to a table.

'He's gonna auction Mrs Battersby. Highest bidder gets her,' Loxton said.

'Don't that beat all?' Corey said, cutting up his bacon.

'Sure does. We're gonna have to pay him his commission,' Loxton went on.

'How much?' Corey asked quickly.

'Ten per cent of what he sells her for.' Loxton poured himself a fresh cup of coffee.

Blade Harris, Mike Day and Jess Garfield were on their way up to Shacktown. It had come to Harris, as they were riding away from the fight at the cabin, that that was where Loxton might be taking her.

'That Loxton, he's gonna die real slow,' Harris said. 'Him an' his boys.'

'Yeah, the whole passel of them,' Mike Day added, urging his horse on.

'It ain't far now,' Garfield said. 'Just a couple of miles, an' we're there.'

They went on, the snow rapidly turning to slush under their horses' hoofs. Shacktown appeared below them.

'What's the plan, Blade?' Day asked, as they reined their horses in, on the rise above town.

'We can't go ridin' down an' ask for her back. What Slim an' his boys will have to do is let the auctioneer know he's got something to auction, an' he'll set it up. We'd better find out where she is first off.'

'Who is this auctioneer?' Garfield put in, as he patted his horse's neck.

'A, fella by the name of Jack Hammer. He's the kind of fella you don't want to cross.' Harris hauled out the makings and handed them round, after he had built his own stogie.

'Why's that, Blaze? Is he a mean *hombre*?' Garfield asked, licking the paper.

'Yeah, an' then some.' Harris put a match to his stogie, then tossed it away. 'Two fellas was arguin' with him about a piece of merchandise. He went along to the blacksmith's and took his hammer and killed them fellas with it,' Harris said, drawing on his stogie. 'An' he's built like a mountain,' he finished up by saying.

Jack Hammer lay in the double bed, with a whore on either side of him. His straggly, black beard covered his face. Yawning lazily, he pushed the redhead out of bed. The whore looked up at him, scratched her head and wondered what the hell had happened. Looking up she saw two bare feet coming down in the direction of her head. The whore rolled out of the way. The feet slammed down on the bare wooden floor.

'Watch where the hell yer goin',' she yelled at Hammer. Hammer glanced down at her, and drew back his foot to kick her, but the whore jumped to her feet and ran across the room, out of Hammer's way.

'Go an' git some coffee an' some eats,' he shouted, his massive belly shaking as he roared at the girl.

The whore made a lunge for her clothes.

'You ain't got time for them,' Hammer yelled threateningly.

The whore took them and bolted into the corridor, buck naked, squealing as she went. Her companion, now more than half-awake, sat up in the bed.

'What's goin' on?' she demanded.

'Yer friend's gone for some eats for us,' Hammer told her, over his shoulder. He swilled his face in the water from a bowl on the table. He wiped the water off with a towel and looked round the room. His hammer rested by the wall under the window. He went over to it, and stroked it fondly. The girl gave him a terrified look. Hammer had a temper that was easily roused, and he was pretty fond of swinging that hammer at anybody who upset him.

'Yer all right, honey,' he said, with a silky venom. 'I ain't gonna hurt you, not unless yer friend takes her time with our breakfast. I'm partial to a good fillin' breakfast.'

Picking up the hammer, he swung it round his head, holding it with both hands. The girl in the bed watched the hammer swing round until it became a blur. Hammer chuckled at the girl's fear, then swung it round with one hand.

'Stop it, Jack. Please, stop it,' the girl screamed, her voice full of fear.

Jack Hammer laughed, then let the weapon fall slowly to the floor. He went over to the bed.

'Hell, yer friend's got more guts than you,' he said. Hammer pushed her back into the bed.

The girl did not speak, but her eyes said it all.

Sam came into the hotel and looked things over. He had taken Kate Battersby's food up to her, and was wondering where Jack Hammer had spent the night.

'Seen Jack?' he asked Tom Moran, when he saw him coming into the saloon. Moran was on the payroll and did odd jobs for him.

'Yeah, he took a couple of Big Freda's girls up to his room last night. I guess they're still there,' Moran told him.

'Well, get yourself over there an' tell him we got somethin' that needs auctioning. OK?'

'Right, boss,' Moran said, and went into the slushy street.

Big Freda's place was just opposite Sam's. Moran

rattled on the doors and waited. A few minutes later they were opened by one of the barkeeps.

'What d'ya want?' the barkeep asked.

'Sam wants Jack Hammer,' Moran told him. The barkeep hesitated before slipping the top bolt, 'He wants him now.'

The door opened and Moran went in. The place was still being swept out by the other barkeeps. Big Freda sat in a chair in front of a table; her eyes were red and bleary. Moran reckoned she had had a hard night.

Freda pushed back her greasy black hair and motioned Moran to come across to her.

She was a big woman; twenty stone, with a muddy complexion. She wore a diamond engagement ring on her third finger. The story went that the man who had given it to her called off the engagement when he had sobered up, and Freda had broken his neck with one hand, which was how she came to be in Shacktown.

'What are you doin' in here?' she asked Moran.

'The boss wants Hammer over at his place,' Moran said.

'What does he want him for at this time of the morning?' Freda asked, taking a long pull at her beer.

'I'm only his errand boy,' Moran told her.

'You've got a big mouth, Moran. Now, what does he want Hammer for?' Freda leaned across the table and held Moran's gaze.

'He's got some merchandise he wants auction-ing,' Moran said, and shoved his thumbs into his belt.

'He's upstairs with a couple of girls. Go an' tell him to see me before he goes across to see yer boss. Understand?' Freda drained the glass, then held it up for another.

Moran knew the way. He rapped on the door and waited.

'Yeah? What do you want?' Hammer called out.

'Sam wants to see you about an auction,' Moran called back. 'An' Freda wants to see you before you go over there.'

'What the hell does that bitch want?' came the reply.

'How the hell do I know?' Moran shouted.

'Tell her I'll be down when I finish eating. You hear?'

'I hear,' Moran called back and went downstairs to tell Freda that Hammer would soon be on his way down.

Freda was sinking another glass. 'You told him?' she called out as Moran went through the saloon.

As Moran was squelching across the muddy street, Harris and his men were coming in at the other end of town. They hauled up outside Big Freda's place and got down. They hitched their horses to the rail and went inside.

'We ain't open yet, boys,' the head barkeep said, when he saw them.

'It's OK, Jimmy,' Freda called out from the table.

Harris's face lit up when he saw Freda.

'Freda,' he yelled, 'How've you bin keepin'?'

Freda pushed her chair back from the table and went to greet him, her arms open wide, and a lascivious grin on her face. Her great arms swamped Harris and she planted a kiss on his cheek.

'Yer lookin' damn well, Blade,' she said enthusiastically.

'I'm doin' damn fine, sorta,' he told her. 'These are my *amigos*. Come over here an' say hello, boys.'

Day and Garfield came over to the table.

'Mike Day an' Jess Garfield,' Harris said.

'Hi,' they both said.

'Nice to meet you. Any friend of Blade's is a friend of mine. Let's have some drinks over here,' Freda called out, a huge grin on her face.

A tray of glasses was brought over by the barkeep.

'What are y'doin' here boys?' Freda asked.

'We lost somethin' an' we're tryin' to get it back,' Harris said cagily.

Freda raised her glass. 'OK, Blade, I got it. You don't want word gettin' around yer lookin' for somethin'. That it?'

'Yeah, that's it,' Harris told her.

'Any ideas where yer gonna start looking?'

Freda asked watching Hammer coming down the stairs.

'We figured Slim Loxton might point us in the right direction,' Harris told her.

Freda's eyebrows went up. 'Loxton? What makes you think Loxton is in this neck of the woods?'

'There ain't no place else fer him to go with what he's got on board,' Harris told her.

Freda thought for a moment. Maybe that was why he'd sent across for Hammer. Maybe what Hammer had to sell belonged to Harris and his boys.

'I guess you boys have some lookin' to do, so I won't keep you around here jawin',' she said to Harris.

Harris recognized that it was time to say *adios*. He finished his drink.

'Come on boys, let's make a move.'

Harris's boys got up and headed for the door.

'What did you want?' Hammer asked, flopping down in the chair that Harris had vacated.

'Slim Loxton an' his boys are in town. They got somethin' to sell, an' I want first call on it.'

For a moment, Hammer said nothing. 'That's against auction rules. Everythin' that comes in here for auction's got to go up in public so everybody gits a fair chance.'

. 'I'm not tryin' to break auction rules,' Freda said quickly, leaning across the table.

'Just what are you saying?' Hammer asked, scratching his beard.

'I'm just askin'. Well, I guess you know what I'm askin',' she said.

Hammer thought for a moment. 'Yeah, I know what yer askin'. I might be able to see my way clear to helpin' you.'

'We get each other's drift,' Freda said.

Hammer got up. 'I'll see you after I've seen Loxton, an' let you know how things stand.'

'Thanks, Hammer,' Freda said. 'An' tell Sam to bring her over here. We'll hold the auction in my place. It'll make it easier,' she said knowingly.

'Loxton's upstairs,' Sam told Hammer when he came into the saloon.

Hammer grunted and went up.

'Hi, Hammer,' Loxton said, getting out of his chair.

'Is this what you've got to sell?' Hammer asked, looking Kate Battersby over.

Kate sat on the edge of the bed, looking with some fear at Hammer.

'Yeah, that's what I got to sell,' Loxton said. 'Get up, so the man can see you,' Loxton ordered her.

Kate got off the bed.

Hammer looked her over again, Kate squirmed away from him. Hammer caught her by the arm.

'Keep still so I can get a good look at you,' he shouted at her. 'I figure you'll get a good price for her. If one of the saloons don't buy her, one of the

127

settlers sure as hell will. Auction'll be in a couple of days. I'll put the word out for you. See you around.'

'See you around,' Loxton said.

Big Freda was still sitting drinking beer when Hammer got back to her.

'I need a fresh girl up here. Some of these girls are gettin' played out. I'll cut you in for twenty per cent over and above your normal fee,' she said to Hammer.

Hammer shook his head. 'Fifty per cent. If these people know that I'm gonna cheat 'em, they'll lynch me.' The threat was not lost on Freda.

'OK, fifty per cent,' she agreed.

'OK.' Hammer got up and walked out.

TEN

Harry and Brett hit town an hour later. They went over to Sam's place,

'We're lookin' fer a friend of ours, Slim Loxton,' Harry began by saying. 'He's travelling with two other fellas.'

Sam looked them over. 'An' just why are you lookin' for this Slim Loxton an' these two other fellas?' Sam asked, setting down the two whiskeys Harry had asked for.

'It's kinda embarrassing,' Harry told him.

'How embarrassing?' Sam asked them.

'They're travellin' with a woman. My friend's niece,' Harry pointed to Brett. 'They're running away to get married, and my friend ain't too happy with it, are you Brett?'

'Hell no. This fella Loxton just ain't good enough for my niece,' he said, as he sipped at his whiskey.

'He ain't, huh,' Sam replied. 'Well, we ain't got no strangers in here, except you, and it ain't you,' he said with a grin. 'I'll tell you what I'll do. You go an' ask round town, and I'll keep my eyes open in here.'

'That's handsome of you.' Harry drained his glass and led Brett out of the saloon.

'That was a damn fool thing to say,' Brett said, when they got outside.

'Why?' Harry asked him sharply.

'It just was,' Brett replied, as they walked along the boardwalk. They got to the end of the block and looked around.

'Let's try over here,' Brett said, crossing to a saloon on the other side of the street.

Inside, the place was near empty and the barkeep wasn't inclined to answer any questions.

'Let's git out of here. He's got nothing to tell us,' Harry said, when they had finished their drinks.

'Guess you're right,' Brett said, leading the way out.

Sam had watched them go, then he called over one of his barkeeps. 'Go find Hammer, an' tell him to get himself back here pronto.'

The barkeep nodded and went out. He found Hammer in a saloon down the block, passing round word about the auction.

'Sam said to get back right away,' he told Hammer.

'I'll be right over,' the bearded giant said.

He gave a low whistle when Sam told him about the appearance of Harry and Brett.

'They can't be the law,' he said. 'I just wonder who the hell they are?'

'It might be a good idea to go up and ask Slim,' Sam advised him.

'No, I can't shed any light on the matter,' Loxton said at first, but then he remembered something. 'Somebody did some shootin' a while back at Blade Harris an' his boys. It might be them. Find them and ask them.'

Brett and Harry came out of the café, having just filled themselves up with hot food and hot coffee.

'Where do we go now?' Brett asked Harry, who was picking his teeth with a matchstick.

'We'd better just keep on asking.' Harry spat out a piece of food that had been stuck in his teeth. Both men looked up and down the slushy street. They walked along to the next saloon.

'Hi, boys,' a voice behind them said. Harry was about to say something when he felt the gun in his ribs.

'Just keep quiet and keep walkin' 'til we say otherwise,' Hammer said to them. They went along the street until they came to an alley.

'Up here,' Hammer said.

They walked down the alley until they came to a disused barn. One of the two men with Hammer pushed the door open. Hammer motioned them to go inside. The place was dark. Picking up a lamp, Hammer lit it.

'You've bin acting pretty nosy,' Hammer said, when they had backed Harry and Brett up against a wall.

'We've just been trying to get a line on this fella's niece,' Harry said.

'Hogwash,' Hammer spat out, cocking his gun. 'Now, let's have the truth fellas. We ain't got all day.'

'That's the truth,' Brett answered.

'OK, if it's gonna be like that, it's gonna be like that,' Hammer said. 'Tie 'em up.'

One of the men came forward and took a rope off a peg in the wall, then tied both men up.

'Let's try agin, shall we?' Hammer said.

'We've already told you,' Brett persisted.

'Yer last chance,' Hammer said to them.

This time neither man said anything.

'OK, it's fine by me,' Hammer said, holstering his gun.

He took a whip from a stall and uncoiled it. He grabbed Harry by his shirt and flung him against a post.

'Tie him to the post,' he ordered one of his men.

The rope was passed round Harry's body and he was fastened to the post.

'Rip his shirt off,' Hammer said.

Harry's shirt was ripped off.

A second later, the whip whistled through the

air, and bit into Harry's skin. Harry strained against the ropes. He bit his lips to keep in the scream; his whole back was a sea of red-hot pain. The whip came down again and again, and each time Hammer asked the same questions.

'All right,' Brett called out, watching Harry writhing against the ropes, 'I'll tell you.'

'Now we're getting somewhere.' Hammer sounded disappointed that Brett had decided to talk. He stood up close to Brett, holding the bloody whip under his nose.

'It's like this. They've kidnapped Mrs Kate Battersby,' Brett began by saying. 'Fred Battersby has offered a reward for her safe return, and we aim to collect on it.'

'Now, start at the beginning and tell us all about it – especially the reward part,' Hammer said.

Hammer watched Brett's face for a minute, undecided whether to believe him or not. The silence stretched.

'I'm gonna see what Sam says. Keep them here until I get back,' he told his men.

Instead of going back to Sam, Hammer went across to see Big Freda. Big Freda had a ham sandwich in her hand. She fed it into her mouth and looked up at Hammer.

'Do you reckon he was tellin' the truth?' she asked him.

Hammer thought for a moment. 'I don't know,

Freda. He might have bin, but he might not.'

'I guess there's only one thing to do,' Freda said. 'You go an' ask her.'

Kate Battersby heard someone coming up the stairs. So far she had not managed to think of a way of getting out of the mess she was in.

Loxton had gone out for some air, leaving Corey to get a drink in the bar. Webb had gone to the doc's to get his leg fixed up.

The door opened and Hammer came in. He stood at the end of the bed, looking down at her.

'Some fellas came looking fer you. They said yer husband has put up a reward, just to make sure he gets you back all right. Is that likely to be right?'

Kate almost jumped out of bed. Her husband was still alive.

'Yes, that's likely to be right, but only if I'm unharmed. If you kill me, my husband will hunt you down through hell and back.'

'How much is he likely to put up?' Hammer demanded.

'$2,000,' Kate replied. 'We've got the biggest ranch in the valley.'

Hammer whistled.

'That's the hell of a lot of money,' Freda said, when Hammer told her.

'If she's right then he's gonna come up with more money than we could in this town,' Hammer went on.

Freda thought it over then nodded her head.

'Yeah, you're right, but what can we do? Loxton's gonna find out, the folks in this town are gonna find out. All that extra money,' she said greedily.

'But that don't answer our question,' Hammer said.

'Give me some time to think about it,' Freda said to him, picking at the crumbs on her plate,

'OK,' Hammer said. 'But what about her?' He gestured to the saloon across the street.

'You put her wise to her best interests. You get back across the street, an' see she doesn't say a word to anybody else.'

'You don't look like a stupid woman,' he began by saying.

'I'm not a stupid woman,' Kate said angrily.

'Well, smarty pants,' Hammer snapped at her, 'you ain't out of the woods yet. We could just go ahead with the auction an' see how much we get fer you.'

'Somehow, I don't think you will.' For the first time Kate felt that she might be able to get out of the mess she was in. 'My husband will find me, no matter where I am, and no matter how long it takes. He'll pay more for getting me back to him than you'll get for auctioning me in this back-of-nowhere.'

Hammer glared at the woman. 'Maybe yer right, but don't count on it an' go shootin' yer mouth off to Loxton. Understand?'

'I understand,' Kate told him, with a growing feeling of confidence.

'I'll be back later.' Hammer turned and headed for the door.

'When you come back make sure you've got something decent to eat and some decent coffee,' Kate told him.

Hammer slammed the door behind him as he went out.

Barney Webb hobbled out of the doc's office and took a deep lungful of fresh air. He sure felt good now that he had seen the doc and got his leg cleaned up.

On the boardwalk, he stopped suddenly, and looked across the street. His lips curled back in a snarl. His hand dropped to his gun, then he thought better of it. He watched as Mike Day continued along the boardwalk, oblivious to his presence.

If Mike Day was in town, then so were the others, he reasoned. He followed Day along the street, but kept to his own side. He watched as Day pushed the batwings back, and went into the saloon. Standing just inside the doorway, Webb watched the man cross the floor. Day went over to one of the soiled doves.

They exchanged a few words, then went upstairs. Webb pushed through the batwings and followed them up.

Jack Corey was just pulling up his trousers.

The soiled dove he had been sporting with was standing by a window, getting her breath back. Corey looked up as the door opened.

'Day,' he called in surprise. He reached for his gun, but it was too far away for him to reach it.

'Howdy.' Day gave a smirk as he reached for his own gun.

'You bastard,' Corey shouted. The whore by the window screamed and threw herself to the floor. She then found herself dragged to one side by a newcomer to the party. There was the sound of a shot. Mike Day crumpled and fell, his spine cut in two by Barney Webb's bullet.

'Glad you were passing,' Corey said as Webb came into the room.

'I saw this sidewinder when I was outside. I guess Blade Harris and Garfield are in the neighbourhood,' he said.

'That means we'd best find them,' Corey said. 'Where's Slim?'

'Still down at Sam's place, I guess.'

'We'd best get down there, then,' Corey told him. 'Here, this is something extra for you.' Corey gave the girl an extra ten-dollar bill.

Loxton showed no surprise at the news his men brought him.

'OK. Let's get them found so we can bury them.'

'Any idea where Harris and his pal Garfield might be?' Loxton asked one of the whores in the saloon where the shooting had taken place.

'I think they're down in the bathhouse gettin' cleaned up.'

Blade Harris and Jess Garfield were just getting lathered up. They'd ridden long and hard without getting near any clean water, so they figured they'd take advantage of the opportunity to get the trail dirt out of their hides while their *amigo* was sporting with a whore.

Harris sank down in the tub of hot water until it covered his hairy body. Then he took a tablet of soap and rubbed it into his body until the lather started to come up.

Beside him, in the next tub, Garfield was scooping the water over his hair. The door opened quietly.

'What are you gettin' cleaned up for boys? You ain't goin' anywhere except your funerals,' Loxton said, holding his gun on them.

Both men looked up.

'Time to say *adios*, fellas,' Jack Corey said, firing the first shot.

Garfeld made a snatch for his gun, but Loxton put a bullet in him.

Barney Webb gave them one shot each. Slowly, they slid down in their tubs, the water turning scarlet as they did so.

'Well, at least they died cleaner than they lived,' laughed Loxton.

Marlene had lain awake in her room all night,

fretting about the way she had been treated. It was all Kate Battersby's fault. When they had auctioned her – and Sam would probably buy her, and work her in one of his saloons – she would be his top attraction.

Marlene knew that she was past her best, and that would mean only one thing: a steady slide down the ladder into the gutter. If Sam didn't buy Kate, he would get rid of Marlene anyway. With Kate out of the way she'd buy herself a little time.

She got up from her untidy bed, and looked at herself in the mirror. The lines were there and were getting deeper. She flung the mirror to the floor and went upstairs.

Kate heard heavy footsteps on the stairs and the creaking of floorboards. The handle turned and Marlene came into the room.

'Hi,' Marlene said. Her voice was so thick, that at first Kate thought that she was drunk. Then she realized that she was not.

'Just come up to see how you were doin',' Marlene came into the room, her right hand hidden behind her skirt.

'I'm doing OK,' Kate said, a cold feeling coming over her as Marlene's step became more purposeful. Kate pushed herself up on the bed as Marlene came towards her.

'I've got somethin' for you,' Marlene said.

'Thanks,' Kate said, as she started to feel apprehensive.

From behind her skirt Marlene brought out the scissors. The light reflected on the blades. Kate scrambled off the bed as Marlene lunged at her. The blade missed her face, but Marlene's weight carried her forward and the blade sank into the pillow.

Kate hit the floor. She lost her balance as she tried to get up, and rolled towards the door. Marlene tugged the scissors free of the pillows.

Overbalancing, Kate fell backwards as she tried to scramble to her feet. Marlene was turning and coming towards her, the scissors ready to plunge into Kate.

'What the hell's goin' on here?' Jack Hammer demanded.

'I'm gonna kill the bitch,' Marlene screamed.

'No, you ain't,' Hammer bawled.

Kate half-raised her arms to protect herself from Marlene's vicious lunge. Then Marlene stiffened and Kate heard a sound like an eggshell cracking. Marlene collapsed, blood pouring out of the back of her head. Hammer stood behind her, slowly lowering the blacksmith's hammer.

'Git her out, and git her buried,' Sam told Hammer when he came to tell him about Marlene.

Then he went to see Freda.

'OK,' Hammer said. 'You thought any more about, them fellas in the ol' barn?'

Freda fed another sandwich into her mouth. 'Yeah, the woman's tellin' the truth. I think we can cut our losses with her.'

Hammer's brows furrowed up. 'How's that?'

'What kinda shape is them two in?' she asked with some difficulty as she chewed on the sandwich.

'That fella we let some blood out of, he's strong, so he's gonna be all right. That smart-dressed fella, I reckon he's a fair hand with a gun.

'You reckon he can shoot, then?' Freda asked, wiping her mouth with the back of her hand.

'Sure. That piece he's wearin', it's seen some work. His pal ain't as good, but he can handle himself, I reckon,' Hammer said.

'Good, we can kill two birds with one stone,' Freda mused.

'How's that?' Hammer asked.

'Get down to the barn, clean them fellas up. Tell them it was a mistake. Bring them down here. Tomorrow, them and Loxton can settle their differences. We can ride out with Mrs Battersby, an' the auction money, then turn her over to her husband and collect the reward.'

Hammer was impressed. 'That's a great idea.'

'Yeah, ain't it?' Freda said, with a self-satisfied grin.

Hammer went down to the old barn, and told the two men who were guarding Harry and Brett to go and get themselves a drink.

'All right fellas, it's all bin a mistake. No hard feelin's?' he asked them.

'Sure, no hard feelin's,' Brett told him, as they helped Harry to his feet. They took him and laid him face-down in the straw.

Hammer filled up a bucket with cold water, and threw it over Harry's back.

'You crazy bastard,' Harry yelled, as the water swept the blood and some of the skin off his back.

'Like I said, I'm real sorry. I was just checkin' your story with Mrs Battersby,' Hammer told him. 'Anyway, Loxton an' his pals are out of town 'til tomorrow. So why don't you come down to Big Freda's place 'til they're in town again. They won't be too long.'

Harry pushed himself up on his elbow and looked at Brett.

Brett shrugged, 'I don't see why not. Maybe we can get a doctor to took at Harry's back.'

'OK,' Hammer said. 'We'll see about getting you a doctor.'

They got Harry to his feet. Hammer threw a blanket over his shoulders. They supported him while they got him down to Big Freda's place. Freda was sitting in the corner, drinking a beer.

'Hi, boys,' she greeted them as they came in. 'Sorry about the misunderstanding.'

As Hammer went out of the door, Big Freda called a barkeep over and had Harry taken upstairs. They eased him face-down on the bed and waited for the doctor. Freda sent down for a bottle and some glasses.

'I'm sure sorry about this,' she told Brett, as they waited for the whiskey and the doc.

'That's all right, just so long as my friend gets a doctor,' Brett said, wondering what her game was. 'Where's Loxton? He has something that belongs to me and my friend, and we want it back.'

'What kinda somethin'?' Freda asked.

'I would have figured your boys would have told you,' Brett said, as she went over to the door to let in the barkeep with the whiskey and the glasses.

'Well, yer gonna have to take it up with him when him an' his boys get back.'

Loxton and his boys were in the upstairs room at the back where Kate Battersby was being kept. They had a couple of bottles of whiskey and a couple of soiled doves with them. They were going over what had happened in the bath-house. Kate could hear them. Her skin crawled as they hashed and rehashed the story of the slaughter.

Then she heard one of the barkeeps come in. 'Hammer's gettin' the auction fixed up. They're gonna auction her in the saloon downstairs,' he said.

Kate pressed herself hard against the mattress and bit her lip.

*

The pain in Harry's back had burned itself down as the doc rubbed in the ointment.

'Jes' stay where you are for a few days an' don't go rollin' over on your back,' the doc told him, wiping his hands with a towel.

Harry groaned and pushed himself up so that he could see the doctor.

He was a small, tubby man with white hair. Harry figured him to be sixty or so.

'I'd best be going to collect my fee from Big Freda,' he said.

'Say Doc, you ever heard of a fella called Mort Jackson? Maybe a barkeep or something like that?' Harry asked.

The doctor hesitated for a moment, 'Sure I know of Mort. He's a barkeep down at the Big Nugget. Why? Is he a friend of yours?'

'Not exactly. An *amigo* of mine asked me to look out fer him, if I ever got out this way,' Harry replied. 'Ask Freda to send me some food up will you? An' ask Brett to come in here.'

'Anythin' you say,' the doctor answered, and closed the door. Harry heard him going down the stairs.

A while later he heard Brett's steps coming up, When Brett came in, he was carrying a plate of food.

'That looks good,' Harry said, as Brett put down

the tray on the table beside the bed.

'How are you feelin' now?' Brett asked him, You look a mite better than when that whip was comin' down on yer back.'

'I'm feelin' a damn sight better. It might have been that hammer coming down on my skull,' Harry said with feeling.

'That's the way to look at it.' Brett picked up a beef sandwich and started to eat it.

'Hey, go easy on that stuff of mine,' Harry growled, reaching for a sandwich.

'Sorry partner,' Brett said between mouthfuls. He picked up the coffee-pot and started to fill out a mug for Harry.

'Thanks, *amigo*,' Harry said, taking the mug and drinking from it.

'That doc that was in here. He knows Mort Jackson,' Harry said.

'Sure. He was the barkeep Hal Roberts was talking about. The doc say where he was?'

'Just down the block. He's working in there as a barkeep. I reckon we should go an' see him, just as soon as we can,' Harry said, taking a long drink from the mug.

'It seems the best thing we can do.' Brett refilled his own mug. 'Maybe, he'll have an idea where Kate Battersby is.'

They finished eating in silence, then Harry pushed himself up and swung off the bed.

'You feel fit enough to do this? Brett asked.

'Sure I feel like doing this,' Harry told him, standing unsteadily for a moment.

'Well, you don't look too good,' Brett said, draining his mug, and getting up.

'Let's get down to that saloon before Mort Jackson dies of old age,' Harry said.

'Anythin' you say.' Brett followed his *amigo* out of the room.

From the corner of the saloon, Freda watched them go out.

'We're lookin' for Mort Jackson,' Harry said, leaning against the bar when they got down there.

The barkeep ran his rheumy eyes over them.

'Yer search has been rewarded,' he said wiping a glass.

'Fill up two more glasses,' Harry said, as Brett leaned on the bar alongside him.

'Comin' up, boys,' Jackson told them, as he put the glasses under the beer tap. He slid the glasses down to the two men, and then picked up their money.

'You boys in town fer anythin' in particular?' he asked them.

'An *amigo* of ours from down the trail said you might be able to help us. We're lookin' fer somebody,' Harry said.

'You lookin' fer anybody in particular or just anybody?' Jackson wiped off the counter top.

'Somebody in particular,' Brett replied, taking

the top off his beer. 'A woman-friend of ours.'

'There's some of them in this saloon.' Jackson folded up his cloth and laid it on the counter. 'This somebody got a name or is it a secret?'

'She's got a name.' Brett watched Jackson's face carefully.

'An' what would that be?' Jackson asked.

'Kate Battersby. We reckon she's here under some kind of duress. Not of her own free will, if you know what I mean,' Brett said.

Harry took a drink from his beer and looked round.

'Yeah. I know what you mean. You bounty men?' Jackson asked after he had looked round the saloon.

'In a manner of speaking,' Brett answered.

'Yer bounty men or you ain't bounty men, in a manner of speakin',' Jackson said with a prickly tone in his voice.

'In a manner of speakin' we ain't bounty men. We've just come to take her back to her husband,' Harry said.

The barkeep sighed, 'Yer gonna have yer work cut out,' he said watching the door.

'You know where she is then?'

'I could make it my business to find out,' the old man said.

'How much would it cost us fer you to make it yer business?' Harry asked, leaning over the bar.

'Wal, seein' as how yer doin' it fer an old friend,

147

let's just say I'll trust you to pay what you can afford. We got a deal?'

Brett shook the barkeep's hand. 'We got a deal.'

'One thing I can tell you,' Mort said. 'I hear there's gonna be an auction in Big Freda's place.'

'We'll be back in a couple of hours, an' you can tell us if it's right or not,' Brett said.

'OK,' Mort replied, as they went through the door.

'We're gonna have to get her out of wherever she is,' Harry said, as they walked along the boardwalk.

'Got any idea as to how?' Brett asked as he pulled out the makings and started to build a stogie.

'Not right off,' said Harry.

'Well, we'd better start thinking,' Brett said, leaning against a hitch rail, and lighting his stogie.

The two men leaned against the hitch rail for a spell, just watching the town. Then Harry yawned.

'I'm feelin' mighty tuckered out. I guess I'm not over that whipping them boys gave me. I'll just go an' rest up for a spell. I'll see you back in the saloon in a couple of hours,' Harry said, and he headed for the hotel.

'I'll see you then,' Brett said.

Harry walked along the street to the hotel. His body was beginning to burn up as he went. He got

148

on to the porch, and walked up the stairs, holding on to the rail tightly. Harry unlocked the door and fell across the bed, his back a sea of fire.

The first thing he saw when the flames of his burning cabin had cleared, was Charlie rigging his fishing pole ready to go down to the creek to do some fishing with him. Then he saw Shirley looking into the mirror, and brushing back her hair. Then it was all gone, with the stallion pawing at the air, his hoofs covered in blood.

'Are you all right, pardner?' Brett was standing over him looking worried.

'Yeah, I'm fine,' Harry told him, pushing himself up on the bed. His face was damp and streaked with sweat. 'Yeah, I'm fine,' he repeated.

'You sure don't look it,' Brett said, sitting on the chair by the bed. 'In fact, you look damn bad. I got worried when you didn't show up at the saloon.'

'I ain't that bad.' Harry sat up and got off the bed. His legs shook and he felt the fever in his body.

'Feel like somethin' to eat?' Brett asked him.

Harry thought for a moment, then decided it couldn't make him feel any worse.

'Sure, why not?' Harry swilled his face and wiped it with a towel.

'Let's take a walk down to Big Freda's place and take a look at it?' Brett said after they had eaten.

They walked across the muddy street, and went

into the saloon. Being mid-morning, it was nearly empty. When they got down there, a fresh set of barkeeps was on, and Big Freda's chair was vacant. Brett went up to the bar and ordered a couple of beers. They looked the place over while the beers were being pulled.

'I hear you're having an auction in here,' Brett said, as the beers were being served.

'Yeah,' the barkeep said, gathering in the coins, 'it should be pretty full in here tonight. You look like a gambling man. There'll be plenty of games being played and plenty of money changing hands.'

'Sweet music to my ears,' Brett smiled.

'Why don't you stop in for a few hands?' the barkeep went on.

Brett pretended to consider it for a moment, then said, 'I guess we might do at that. What do you say, partner?'

'Can't think why not. There ain't gonna be too much else to do,' Harry replied, taking a drink from his mug.

'The barkeep moved away. Harry watched him go.

'Should be just a few hours before they get started,' Harry said.

'Yeah, just a few hours,' Brett agreed.

Kate Battersby had a visit from Hammer, who told her that she was going to be auctioned that night. Kate thought about her future. She felt an angry desperation raging though her. Why didn't somebody come for her?

'You'd better eat this,' Hammer told her, handing her the tray.

For a wild moment, Kate thought about throwing it in his face, and making a run for it, but she knew she would not get far.

'Glad you've given up even thinkin' about it,' Hammer said, with a laugh, as she started to eat.

Kate looked at him sharply. The temptation to throw it in his face rose up again. She suppressed the thought. Hammer laughed again and went out. She heard him lock the door behind him.

Across the way, Harry and Brett walked into the saloon and went up to the bar. Mort came down and took his order.

'Two beers,' Harry said, reaching into his pockets for the coins.

'She's in an upstairs room over Big Freda's. It's just across the way,' Mort said, as he scooped up the coins.

Brett slid a twenty-dollar bill over the bar.

Harry said nothing until the barkeep had moved away. 'We're gonna have to move mighty quick.'

'Like as soon as we've finished these beers,' Brett said quietly.

'Any idea how?' Harry asked, watching the other customers in the saloon.

'The best thing we can do is go over there and see how things stand,' Brett said, wiping his mouth.

'I guess so,' Harry replied.

'Can you think of anything better?' Brett asked.

For a moment Harry thought about it. 'No, I guess I can't,' he said, slowly.

'Let's go down the livery and get our horses and a spare one for Mrs Battersby,' Brett said.

They went down to the livery stable together.

'Come fer yer horses, boys?' the old man with the corncob pipe asked.

'Yeah,' Harry told him. 'We'd like a spare, if you've got one.'

'I can fix you up with a spare,' the old man said. 'But it'll cost you.'

'I'll pay if it's worth it,' Harry said.

The liveryman gave him a sideways look. 'I figured you'd know something about horses.'

They walked down the aisle between the stalls until they came to their horses. Both animals had been well cared for and well fed.

'I've got a black I can let you have for ten dollars,' the liveryman told Harry, as he led the mare out of the stalls. Harry ran his hands over the mare's flanks.

'Nice animal,' he said. 'I'll give you ten dollars for her.'

He pulled out his billfold and peeled off the money, plus what he owed the liveryman for looking after their horses.

'Can you see yer way clear to throwin' in a blanket and saddle?' Brett asked.

The liveryman thought for a moment, then said, 'I don't see why not. There's some at the back and the owners won't be riding anywhere again.' He took the pipe out of his mouth, and spat into the dust of the livery stable.

Harry and Brett saddled up their own horses, and waited outside while the liveryman saddled the black mare.

'Now what do we do?' Harry asked.

'We get ourselves some matches,' Brett replied with a smile.

'Some matches? What do we need them for?' Harry asked with a look of surprise.

'To start a fire with. That saloon's gonna take some burning in weather like this,' Brett told him. 'And we can't get Mrs Battersby out if everybody's in there.'

The liveryman came out of the barn, leading the mare. The two men got mounted, and Harry held the spare horse. They rode down to Big Freda's place and hitched their horses across the street. Brett led the way in through the batwing doors. Freda was leaning against the bar when they got in there.

She turned when the batwing doors creaked open. 'Glad to see yer up an' about,' she said to Harry when they came up to the bar.

'So am I,' Harry said, as neutrally as he could.

'Just so there's no hard feelin's, this one's on the house,' she said, signalling for one of the barkeeps.

'Beer all right?' she asked them.

'Beer's fine,' Brett said.

The barkeep came down to their end of the bar. He pulled them two beers and moved away.

'It seems pretty slack in here, right now,' Brett said.

'It'll liven up when we start the auction. I figure Hammer told yer friend about it?'

'He sure did,' Harry said, through gritted teeth.

'You don't seem too happy with the way Hammer treated you,' Freda said with a sly grin.

'Harry ain't too pleased,' Brett put in.

As she spoke, a bunch of men came into the saloon.

'Oh well, it takes all kinds,' she said with a sarcastic sneer, and walked down to the other end of the bar.

'Where do you reckon Loxton an' his boys are?' Harry asked.

'Upstairs, keeping an eye on Mrs Battersby, I reckon,' Brett told him. 'We're gonna have to light ourselves a bonfire.'

'How do you reckon we go about it?' Harry looked round the saloon.

'I figure there's a storeroom of some kind on the other side of that door,' Brett said, pointing to a door in the back wall. 'This place is pretty well empty, so I reckon we can get on the other side of that door and get that fire going. Then we find Mrs Battersby while everybody's trying to put the fire out. And we can take care of Loxton and his boys,' Brett said with a grin.

'Can't you think of anything a mite less risky?' Harry, asked his friend.

'No. Can you?' came the short answer.

'No, I can't,' Harry replied.

A flurry of noise from the far end of the bar attracted their attention.

'Looks like we're gonna have a singsong,' Brett said, as Freda, the pianist and the newcomers to the saloon gathered round the piano, and started to beat out a song. The few drinkers from the tables joined them.

'I reckon this is the best chance we're gonna get,' Brett said, putting down his empty glass. Harry followed him as he headed for the door.

The door opened into a storage room and a set of stairs. In the corner by the wall stood some opened packing cases with paper and wood shavings strewn around them. Brett took out the matches and scraped one along the wall. The light flared, and he dropped it in among the shavings. The flames started to lick at them.

'Let's go and find Mrs Battersby,' Brett said as he headed for the stairs.

Harry followed. Behind him, he could hear the crackling of the wood.

At the top of the flight of stairs, they came on to a dimly-lit landing. A door opened suddenly, throwing out a shaft of light. A soiled dove came out pulling her robe round her buxom figure. She looked at the two men and opened her mouth to scream. Harry clapped his hand over it, and hauled her into the corridor.

'Where's Kate Battersby?' he demanded, pushing her up against the wall.

'She ain't gonna tell you with yer hand over her mouth,' Brett said, looking round.

The girl's eyes were open wide, and she looked real frightened with Harry's .45 under her nose.

'Just tell us what we want to know,' Harry told her. 'Do you understand?'

The girl nodded her head furiously. Harry moved his hand.

'She's in that room there.' The whore nodded towards the room at the end of the corridor.

'Let's go,' Brett said, waggling his gun in the direction of the room. When they got there, the whore knocked softly on the door.

'Damn it,' Harry snarled impatiently, then reached over and turned the key. The room was almost dark. In the middle Kate Battersby was crouched on the floor watching them come in.

'Get yer stuff, lady, we're in a hurry. This saloon's about to burn down,' Harry said to her.

'Who are you?' Kate asked them.

'We're the fellas that are going to take you back

to your husband,' Brett said quickly.

'You mean it's true? Fred's still alive,' Kate Battersby gasped.

'Yeah,' Harry cut in. 'He's alive, but we won't be if you don't hurry.'

At his side, the soiled dove suddenly screamed. A scream that echoed through the saloon.

'That does it,' Harry said, as Kate Battersby got to her feet and grabbed her coat.

Brett went out first, his gun ready. Beside him, Harry pushed the whore forward, with Kate Battersby crushed in between him and the other woman.

As Brett got into the corridor a door opened, and Barney Webb came out holding his gun.

Brett put a bullet in his heart. Webb crashed back into Jack Corey, who was screaming with rage. Brett and Harry pushed their way towards the head of the stairs. The soiled dove forced her way out of the line of fire as she saw the smoke curling up towards them.

'Keep goin',' Harry shouted.

He turned in time to see Jack Corey struggling over Webb's body, his gun ready. Harry steadied himself and shot him down. Corey staggered into the room, his hand covering his face. Loxton tossed a shot over his shoulder, clipping Harry's ear.

Yelling, Harry put his hand to his ear, and threw a shot at Loxton. Loxton jumped behind the door and slammed it shut.

A shout from Brett caused Harry to turn. 'The place is burning faster than I figured it would,' the gambler hollered.

Smoke and flames were curling up the stairs. Harry could hear shouting from below. He pulled Kate towards him.

'We'll have to go through the window,' he shouted to Brett.

They ran back to the room. The door was flung open, and Loxton came out shooting. His bullets went wide and Brett shot him through the head.

When they got into Kate Battersby's room, Harry went to the window and looked down into the yard. He pushed the window open.

'Got a head for heights?' he asked her.

'I think so,' she replied.

'Well, there ain't no other way out of here,' Brett said. 'Harry, you help the lady to lower herself on to the privy. I'll keep things clear out here.'

Kate Battersby started to climb over the sill with Harry holding on to her.

'You there?' he shouted to her.

'Almost,' she said. 'Let go of my hand now.'

Harry let go. He heard her land on the roof of the privy. Sticking his head out of the window, he could see that she was all right.

'Everything all right back there?' he yelled to Brett.

'Fine,' Brett shouted to him. 'You get yourself out of that window. I'll be right behind you.'

Harry followed Kate down on to the roof of the privy.

'We'd best be gettin' out of here,' he told her. 'This roof doesn't feel too safe.'

He jumped down from the roof and waited for Kate. As he got down, he saw Brett coming out of the window.

'Come on. Half the town's in that saloon,' Brett said.

They ran out of the yard, and out into the alley that went alongside the saloon until they reached the corner. Everything looked pretty confused. Hammer stood on the edge of the crowd yelling orders to get the fire put out.

'Reckon we could make it?' Brett asked, throwing a glance to the three horses on the other side of the street.

'We're gonna have to be quick,' Harry said.

The three of them ran across the slushy street. The horses were getting nearer and nearer. Harry untied the leathers. The others did the same. They climbed into the saddles. Hammer saw them and threw a shot their way.

Harry turned in his saddle and threw one back. Hammer caught it in the chest. He spun and fell into the slush.

The three of them rowelled their horses and rode out of town.

*

'I'm damn glad to be out of that,' Brett said, after an hour's hard riding.

It took them five days to get back to Beaver and Fred Battersby.